Jonathon and Dee.

A Tale of The Feyra.

George R. Mead

E-Cat Worlds Press

Jonathon and Dee

LCCN 2010937982

Mead, George R.
Jonathon and Dee/
George R. Mead.
p. cm. – (A Tale Of The Feyra; Tale 1)
ISBN-13 978-0-9817446-3-6
1. Fantasy. I. Title. II. Series.

E-Cat Worlds established its publishing program as a reaction to the large commercial publishing houses currently dominating the book industry and the smaller intellectual clones. It is interested in publishing works of fiction and non-fiction that are often deemed insufficiently profitable or commercial or that are not necessarily reflective of literary trends and fads.

E-Cat Worlds, 57744 Foothill Road, La Grande OR 97850
www.ecatworldspress.com
SAN 255-6383

In the middle of nowhere - Creativity.

First Edition:
Printed in the United States of America

From Grandeville.

Portal
Lair
Search
Not Again
And Again.
Magiwitch
Rebirth
Offspring
Holiday

A Tale of The Feyra

Jonathon and Dee

Nonfiction

A History of Union County
The Ethnobotany of the California Indans

I was born.

I lived.

I died.

Well, two out of three aren't too bad
George R. Mead.

Chapter One

So, This Is How Things Begin?

A Small House Next To The Ocean.

He woke. All at once.

Just as he always did.

He woke in the beautiful grey dimness that was the start of the day just before the sun came hurtling into the sky and changed everything.

He woke, as he always did, at the moment of the beginning of yet another day. One of many.

He yawned, stretched, joins making crackling sounds, rolled from the bed, and with the fluid grace of a dancer, or perhaps a predator, walked into the kitchen, got a cup of coffee from the coffee maker on the timer, took a sip and looked out the window at the soft orange glow of the sun edging its way up past the not too distant mountain range beyond the nearby ridge. He turned and wandered to the other side of the house, out onto the deck, dropped into a chair, sipped from his cup, inhaled coffee odors and the Pacific Ocean salt air. He felt the gentle ocean breeze drifting past, over the deck and off to the east to greet the rising sun.

Watching the waves curl in and slither up the wide beach, and back down again, he sipped and thought about this or that. And a strange, small poem of a sort popped into his mind from some long ago thing he had read somewhere.

> The Ocean throws upon the sands,
> > Water with a thousand hands.
> And when the restless sea is stilled,
> > The sands are dry,
> > The ocean filled.

And, after awhile, he stood and leaned against the railing and took another sip and stared at the far horizon. And thought that little poem pretty much typified the people. Lots of activity, little accomplishment.

He was neither tall nor short. He was neither fat nor thin. His facial features were even, making him neither handsome nor ugly. Other than having a rather pale complexion, he was simply a quite unremarkable looking individual. He was, in point of fact, that sort of an individual that is seen and forgotten almost immediately. It was exactly the way he liked to be.

So, he leaned, and sipped, and thought.

He thought about the ability of the people to believe in pure nonsense and various types of mythology and to treat all that as some sort of reality.

He laughed, a gentle, soft, almost silent laugh.

He nodded to himself. His family had a long history with some clever folk among those ancestors who had been very shrewd dealers and sellers of this and that to the people in whatever the mode of their times had been. And so, here he was, today, living a life that was often called "well off." He didn't really have to work, unless he felt like doing something like that. So, mostly, he didn't. Work.

Actually, being here at this place was a sort of vacation for him, a time to be by himself.

In the not too long ago past he had traveled, wandered quietly, here and there, spending some time in France, enjoying the cuisine, and visiting those gigantic structures, the cathedrals. The vast interior spaces were interesting with the immense pillars, all tree trunks soaring into the dim incense misty air high above, great monuments to mythology.

He turned away from the ocean view and his contemplation and wandered back into the kitchen for a refill. Stepping to the window, he smiled into the radiant sunshine streaming into the room greeting the day and headed back to the deck to sit and muse about things, feet propped on the railing.

He enjoyed reading, all types of literature, and marveled at the monster industry that was now alive and well, especially the ever expanding vampire genre. It amazed him that one author, Bram Stoker, who had apparently based his fiction on a real monster of a ruler,

Vlad the Impaler, and had then merged bits and pieces of old folk tales with the religious nonsense of his time in his story which had now become such a cash cow with Hollywood's favorite bogeyman, Dracula, paying the way. And now there were TV series and numbers of books running other series of tales. All variations on the same theme.

He thought that it was interesting how all that creativity followed the same basic formula, over and over and over, with minor changes to match various consumer demographics. It was most often the same spooky fellow who haunted the dark and the dark spaces and who had a real hangup about young, nubile and innocent females, mostly, to feast upon, and who, the monster and his created monsters, always met a rather horrible and ghastly end after meeting up with some hero, or heros, wielding wooden stakes, a large hammer, jars of that so-called holy water, and various religious icons that were always Christian but never any of the other belief systems. He nodded to himself. It must be that particular religion's fears of normal Homo sapiens sapiens sexual behavior. They had no idea what the other sub-species did.

He sipped and watched a few seagulls and pelicans drift silently by with barely moving wings as they made their way down the beach. He nodded. Oh well, everyone needs to have a monster of some sort, especially these days.

Maybe he ought to have one, just to have

something to worry about. Maybe he ought to take some time and search the family records just to see if sometime in the past they had one, a monster to worry about. It might be interesting. Of course, maybe it might not be.

He stood, stretched, set his cup on the flat railing, yanked off his t-shirt, checked for anyone looking this way, and vaulted up and over the railing to land with a soft thump on the sand. And started up the beach, just a slow easy run, just a light jog, feet skimming every so lightly over the packed sand at the water's edge.

He was just one of the several, out for a bit of early morning exercise. He breathed deeply and thought that this was ever so very pleasant.

She knew that she had to talk to someone. She knew that she had to ask someone for help. She didn't know what else to do. It was getting worse. But she knew that she wasn't about to seek clinical care. Not for this problem it wasn't. She certainly wasn't interested in getting locked up for observation.

There was no way she would do that, absolutely no way she would talk to someone like that. How could she convince some clinician that she actually had things like that in her house, things that came and went as they pleased, things that were large, things that were that ugly, things that talked to her. Always when she was getting ready for bed or later in the dark of night. No way was she going to allow someone to label her as having paranoia something or other.

Yes! She was pushing the upper bounds of thirty. No! She didn't have a boyfriend. No! She hadn't ever been married. And no, no, no, no, no, no, it didn't have anything to do with her repressed sexual desires or unsatisfied lust, or a wildly out of control imagination It certainly was none of that Freudian sexual nonsense.

It was just something large and ugly that came and went as it pleased. And frightened her, close but not totally out of her wits. At least, not yet.

So, she had to talk to someone and ask them for help, not treatment, although she had no idea what sort of help anyone could actually offer.

She stopped editing her manuscript. Her wild imagination wasn't working right now. She wasn't getting anything accomplished. She stood, stretched, and walked out her side door.

This was a very pleasant spot to have a house. It was quiet. And good place to think and write. It was peaceful, except for that one thing. The few that had been built on this wide bench were very widely spaced apart. All the buildings had been built fairly close to the edge of the wide flat space high above the high tide mark. A few had decks that thrust out over the edge. Her nearest neighbor to the north was one that had a deck with stairs heading south from it and down to the beach. She had a narrow path to a small landing where her stairs wended their way back and forth to the base of the cliff. Others had other systems. All had a magnificent view of the ocean to the west and in the not too far distance the mountains to the east, peeking up and over the nearby ridge. Some good way toward the east the flat land began to rise to that rather high crest over which the access road climbed. That road turned at the base of that ridge and ran parallel to the base with feeder roads perpendicular to it for each of the dwellings.

Her nearest neighbor was a little over a quarter of a mile away along this bluff. She had watched him as she sat on her small balcony when he was taking one of those loose-limbed jogs up and down the beach. When he ran it didn't look like it was work at all unlike many of the others who seemed to have to labor so hard to do the same thing. He had probably been doing this for a long time and those others were merely beginners.

She nodded to herself and headed toward his house. And laughed. She had no idea why she was doing what she was doing, not at all. She was on her way to tell an absolute stranger that she had a large, ugly thing popping in and out of her house. And she had no idea how she could explain why she had decided to ask him for help.

She strolled across the newly mown grass that stretched between the two houses. And wondered if maybe she wasn't losing her mind after all.

Chapter Two.

Surprise.

A Small House Next To The Ocean.
So he had run.
He did. Jog.
Up the beach.
Skimming along with ever so soft footfalls.

And, eventually, as he must always do, the beach terminated at a large rock point thrusting out in the sea, he ran back down the beach, up the stairs, and into the kitchen, after retrieving his coffee cup from the flat porch railing, to refill it. After wiping away the light sheen of sweat from his face and chest with a handy towel, he walked back to the porch, sat, and sipped. And thought, that was very enjoyable, maybe I will do it again, after I finish my coffee. So, he mused about that and other things that his mind had decided to muse about.
Then it happened.
He was interrupted.
Someone had just, ever so gently, knocked on his side door, the outside door.

Now this was an unusual thing to have happen. He rarely had visitors. Here. Certainly not very recently as he counted the passage of time. So he was surprised and thought that it was interesting that someone would do that. He sipped at his coffee and wondered whether he ought to answer that ever so gentle knock at his outside side door. He listened, carefully, for footsteps going away. They didn't go away. They didn't announce themself. The visitor did it again, ever so gently, they knocked.

Curiosity aroused, he stood, pulled on his t-shirt, picked up his cup, and walked casually over to that door just to see who or what might be ever so gently knocking on his outside door. After all, one never knew, did one, in advance, about things like that.

So it was a surprise.

It was the beautiful young woman from next door, from the house over a quarter of mile down the cliff from his, but next door none the less. She was somewhat shorter, so he looked down. "Yes?"

"May I come in?"

He looked at her, very carefully, and nodded. "Do come in." And backed up so she could enter and then led her out to the deck and waved at a chair. "Here?" It was a good spot to sit and talk with visitors, even if they were rare. For this place.

She sat. "Thank you."

He sat, after twisting his chair around so he could see and talk with her comfortably. "Yes?"

"I know that this is an intrusion."

"Yes."

"But I need help."

"Yes."

"And I thought that maybe you could do that."

"Yes."

"Help."

"Yes. Doing?"

"Perhaps I ought to explain."

"Yes."

She stared at him. This was a really strange conversation, if one could call it that. He just sat there. Not a muscle moved, anywhere. He was a statue that ever so carefully watched her and spoke mostly in single word sentences.

She carefully explained.

He nodded. "Call the people police."

She stared at him, explained some more, and wondered at his strange terminology.

"Ummmmmmm."

She added more details.

"I see."

She sat up and stared at him. "You do?"

"Yes. Coffee? I will get it."

"Yes, thank you."

He fetched two cups from the kitchen, his and a new one, both full, and handed her one. "Black."

"Black is good." She sipped.

He sipped. "Why me?" And nodded at her. And

laughed, a soft, gentle laugh. "That was the universal question."

She shrugged. "I have no idea. I really do not know how to explain that. When I stepped out and looked this way, it just seemed like the thing to do." She smiled at him.

He sighed, a very soft sigh. And though, oh well, it had been a rather quite life for a rather long time. He stood, set his cup on the flat railing. "Shall we walk back to your house? Now?"

"Oh!" She bounced to her feet. "Of course." She set her cup next to his.

They walked across the well groomed grass between their two houses. His property was carefully maintained and large enough to have sufficient privacy from any neighbors and potential developers. The side of his property away from her's was a steep rocky slope that dropped down to the beach. No visitors could come from that direction. As they approached her place he saw that it was more modest in size, but also well maintained.

"This visitor always comes at the same time?"

"Yes. At night."

They stopped at her door. He waited for her to open it. "Come in," she said.

He glanced around as he stepped inside. "I will stay until something happens."

She spun around. "All day, all night?"

"Yes."

"What will you do?"

"When?"

"All day and all night."

"Wait."

"While you are waiting?"

"Read something. Drink coffee. Eat something or other. Do you have books, coffee, food?"

"Why yes, of course." She smiled. That was a strange question.

"Problem?"

"Ahhhh, no," She shook her head. "Surprised, just surprised, that's all."

"Ummmm?"

"A perfect stranger knocks on your door and asks you for help. You sigh and say O.K. and let's walk back to your place. And then you say that all you want is something to eat, coffee to drink, and some books to read. So, how come? How come you don't want something else?"

He smiled, a soft, gentle smile. "It is something to do. Something about the rescue of a beautiful young woman. A cliche of some sort in, ummmmm, certain types of literature. I do not require anything else."

She laughed. "You are strange, you know that?"

"Yes."

"And I am nearly thirty-seven."

"Yes. A beautiful young woman."

She blushed.

He sighed, a soft, gentle sigh. And thought to

himself. Oh well.

She gave him a quick tour of the place and entered the kitchen as the last stop. "Coffee?"

"Please."

As they sat and sipped their coffee in her living room, listening to the waves surging onto the beach, she half-turned and asked, "So what do I do? What do you want me to do?" Her eyes jumped from his face and looked in the general direction of the ocean.

"Whatever you usually do. That is what I think you ought to do." He smiled, a soft, gentle smile. "Just that."

"And you? What will you do?"

"Be around. Read a little. Drink some coffee. Have a snack. Wait."

"That's it?" She stared at him. She had expected more, somehow. More action, more preparation, more something. Not just waiting.

"Yes."

"For how long?"

"Long as it takes."

She didn't know what to say or do. So she said, "All night?"

"Yes."

Her cheeks flushed. "I, ah, umm, do not have, eh, overnight guests."

"You are safe. From me. You will never notice that I am around. I am very quiet." He stood, walked back to the kitchen and refilled his cup and headed for the outside door, cup in hand. "Going to walk around for awhile. Don't lock the door, leave some books on the table in the living room. I will look at them later." He gently closed the door behind himself.

So she did what she usually did. And soon forgot that he was there as she worked in her study. Day was turning to dusk before she realized that she had somehow worked right through lunch. Again. For her it was a fairly normal occurrence. Whenever she was writing and the story was flowing forth, she forgot time and her surroundings.

Jumping to her feet, she hurried to the kitchen snapping on lights as she went. Her guest, she now thought of him as her guest, must be hungry and wondering why she had ignored him in such a self-centered way.

She was banging pots and pans around preparing something to eat when he wandered into the kitchen, coffee cup in one hand, book in the other, and looked over her shoulder. "Italian sausage?"

"Yes. Hope you don't mind garlic. Lots of people don't."

"Love it."

"Good." She laughed. "Cause that is all I happen to have at the moment, Didn't think I needed to go food shopping so soon."

"I made more coffee."

"Feel free. Mi casa es su casa."

He twisted around and stared at her. "You shouldn't say things like that."

She shrugged. "Just a saying."

"Ummm."

"Something wrong?"

"Ahhh, ummmm, no. Smells really good."

They ate in comfortable silence. She was surprised that it was, comfortable. He wasn't. When they were done, he stood, took the dishes away and washed them, ignoring her protests. She wasn't used to people doing things like that. He did it, washed the dishes, quickly and efficiently.

Then he walked into her living room, sat down and began to read.

She snapped on the light.

"Forgot," he said. She blinked. The room had been dark.

Sometime later, she called, "Do you need to use the bathroom?"

"No."

"I am going to take a long soak. You sure?"

"Yes."

She walked back, and pointed down the hall. "My bedroom is that door. I made up the bed in the other bedroom."

"Most welcome," he said.

She headed down the hall and began to wonder if she had done something very stupid letting him into her house.

Her eyes popped open, stared into the darkness, well, almost darkness, there was a strange faint light, and peered at the glowing numerals on her bedside clock.

Midnight. The witching hour. Poor time to wake up, she thought, thinking of all those horror movies.

Staring into the almost blackness it seemed to her that something stood there, at the foot of her bed. Slowly, ever so carefully, she pushed herself back and then upright against the wall. It better not be her neighbor thinking that just because she let him stay in her place at night that he could have a friendly little visit. She tried to remember where she had left that large and heavy flashlight.

Something stepped onto her bed and moved close. "From daughter to daughter to daughter," it gurgled.

"The power flows. From daughter to daughter to daughter. He waits. He wants. You! It is time to secure the future!"

It was there again, she could tell it was her unwanted visitor making another call and making no sense at all.

She leaped to her feet. And was slammed up and back, to hang near the wall, feet dangling, arms spread wide, held in place. She was floating, suspended there by something unseen.

The thing leaned close and spoke with a different voice. "I would see what I would see, Princess to this Prince."

Black talons, glistening in that faint light coming from somewhere, lightly touched the side of her face. Then, with gentle precision, sliced her over-sized t-shirt from the neck to the bottom and then along each sleeve. The garment slipped soft sigh to the bed.

Something heavy depressed the bed as a large hand, long fingers, wrapped themselves around the thing's neck and pulled it backward.

"Release me!" snarled the second voice. "Release me, ka'na'ka! You have nothing here. This female is mine. I will have what is mine!"

A voice soft as a summer breeze, chill as the depths of the ocean, hissed, filling the room with its sound, "You may never approach this one again, Messenger thing, and all your kind. This is to be so."

The things vanished. She thumped to the bed. The room was filled with midnight dark.

The light snapped on as he stepped from the open doorway, and held out her robe, eyes looking past her head. He dropped her robe on the foot of the bed. "Here. I made coffee." His other hand held a filled cup. "We need to talk, D. Grant, in the living room." He set her cup on top of the dresser, turned, never looking in her direction, and walked down the hall, and around the corner.

Snatching up her robe, she jumped from the bed,

yanked it on and closed it, waggled the belt into a loose knot, grabbed her cup, took a sip, and followed him.

Two floor lamps cast a soft glow in the room. He was sitting in one of the large chairs, sipping, eyes watching her as she walked in, sat, and took a sip. A stack of her novels sat on the floor next to his chair.

"D. Grant is my nom du plume. I am sorry. I didn't think to introduce myself properly." She frowned at him. "Which I usually do when I meet someone." She cleared her throat. "My real name is Daliera d'Tonis a'Natur. Hardly something to be putting on a book jacket." She waggled her free hand at him. "Don't ask. I really don't know. My parents never told me." She smiled. "I did a search. As far as I can find out, I seem to be the only one." Dark eyes stared at him. "And you?"

"Ah. I am Jonathon Harkerness. I come from a rather, ummm, scattered family." He waggled the hand not holding the cup, loosely, more or less in her direction. "We have, ah, homes, umm, here and there."

He slumped, a little, and sipped, a little, from his cup. "What have you been doing, Daliera, to warrant such nocturnal visitors?"

"Dee! I prefer Dee. Nothing. I write, and am a sorta reclusive type of person. Nothing. Did you see those two things? Do you know why that thing keeps appearing? Do you know what is going on in my house? Do you know anything at all? Especially, do you know why I would ask a total stranger for help? Why?"

He held up one hand, stopping the flow of

questions.

She clamped her mouth shut, teeth banging together, startled by that imperious gesture that had so much command in it.

Chapter Three.

Conversations.

A Small House Next To The Ocean.

"Tell me about yourself, Dee."

"O.K., then it will be your turn."

"Fair enough. Proceed."

She leaned back, took a sip, and told him.

She was the only daughter of an only daughter which is all that she knew about her family. Her parents were always going to tell her "one of these days" but they never had a chance to do that. Their daughter was smart and talented and they had encouraged her to follow her own path. So, that is what she did. Writing.

She had been on a Book Tour. And laughed. "As D. Grant." And then, somewhere in the Midwest she was told. The home where she grew up had burned to the ground. Her parents had died in that fire. The Fire Investigators couldn't find anything to explain the blaze other than, maybe, faulty wiring somewhere in the basement of the house. And that was that.

Between an inheritance, and her income from her already written books, she bought the place where they were now sitting sipping coffee.

She settled back in her chair and looked at him.

"I lost everything in that fire. Your turn, neighbor."

He nodded.

He came from a family that had a tradition of knowing and remembering their ancestral lineage.

"So," he said, "I can recite the whole thing. It was something that each child had to be able to do in case the records were ever destroyed or lost. Neither event has yet occurred. But it is a family tradition."

He smiled, a soft, gentle smile. "My ancestors were, at times, very clever, and through generations saved more than they spent." He laughed, a soft, quiet laugh. "Soooooooo, I do not have to work, or do anything that I do not wish to do." His eyes, a very strange blue, watched her face, a very careful stare. "I read whatever I wish to read. I work if I wish to do that. I wake up in the morning and watch the day start. I drink coffee." He held up his full cup. She hadn't noticed when he had refilled it.

He took a sip. "And, I help beautiful damsels in distress. Ummmm, if they should happen to ask."

"And," she added, "you are a very quiet person."

"Yes. One might say that, I suppose."

"What did you study in college."

"Nothing."

"Nothing?"

"I was tutored."

"In?"

"Family history, as I mentioned. Literature. The cultural history of many." He waggled his free hand

and took a sip. "And on and on and on and on."

Then he told her all about this travels, here and there, in great detail. And talked about this and that. And on and on and on and on. Waiting for the sun to come up.

"O.K.!" She sat up, breaking into his long, long monolog, and tried to read his expression. It was a failed effort. There was no expression. "What is going on? Here? In here, my home? Why me? Do you have any idea?" She frowned at him. "I keep asking and you keep not answering! Do you know?"

He nodded.

"What!" she snapped. "Oh! Sorry. Nervous reaction. I am very nervous." She pointed at her bedroom. "About whatever that was all about."

"Yes."

"So?"

"Ummmmm. You are in danger, it appears."

"That is certainly an understatement if I ever heard one. From what? Those things?"

"The first one that spoke, no. The other voice that spoke, yes. The one who interfered, no."

"So, you do have some idea about what that was all about, don't you?" She was beginning to feel like the heroine in one of her many books. It was not a comfortable thought. She laughed. "So I am a damsel in distress?"

"Yes."

"How come?"

"I do not know. It is something about you, I think." He watched her carefully, a slow, appraising, searching look.

"Me?" She tugged her robe closed at the neck.

"Yes."

"So what were those things? In there?" She pulled the belt tighter.

"The first was a Messenger thing. It gave you a message. The second voice was the one who sent it. He gave you a message. He wants you. I think that what he wants you wouldn't be interested in giving. The other, ummmmm, figure, merely barred either of them from ever returning again. To, ah, here."

She leaned forward and glared at him. "And what was that other whatever it was that appeared behind that, erm, messenger with the two voices?"

"Oh, that."

"Right! That!"

He stood and headed for the kitchen and filled his cup. He turned, leaned back against the counter and watched her stomp into the room, forgetting to be nervous.

"Speak!"

He leaned back a little more. "Ah um, that was, ummm ah, a friend, ah, in a manner of speaking, ummmm, so to speak."

She grabbed his arm and then jerked her hand away. His arm was rock hard and felt cool. "Oh! Sorry. Shouldn't have done that." She stared into his eyes.

"Don't leave."

He turned and looked out the window. "I do not wish to frighten you, ummmm ah, any more than you are already." He nodded. "Now."

Then he turned back, a single swift movement. She jumped back.

"Of course you ought to be frightened and very cautious. The one that was responsible for sending that Messenger thing will not stop. You should know that. That one will not stop, not now, not ever. That one sounded very determined. That one wants you whether you know the reason, or reasons, why."

"But, why me?"

"That is the universal question, isn't it?" He turned back and watched the sun crawling its way into a new day. "A very pretty sight isn't it?"

He turned back, slowly, the sun poured through the window highlighting him in a golden glow. "I think that one wants an offspring. And you have been chosen to do that. That one has decided that, no, that one wants you to be the female that gives birth."

"Well, maybe I do not want to be the female that gives birth for someone that sends ugly to my bedroom!"

She spun away. "Come with me. Please? I need to get dressed."

He straightened up. "I will wait here."

"NO!" she snapped. "I am afraid to be in there, alone."

He frowned. "You want me to watch you get dressed?"

She laughed. "You can close your eyes. Although you already saw most of what there is to see already."

He followed her as she strode away. And wondered. And thought to himself, ah well.

He stood in the doorway as she banged wall closets open. "I will close my eyes."

She laughed again. And said, mostly to herself as she selected what she thought would be appropriate garb for a damsel in distress. "How can things get so strange so fast?" Then she decided jeans and other attire would be the best choices.

"I ask myself that same question every once in a long while." He leaned against the door jamb, eyes tightly closed.

"You heard?"

"Yes." He heard the soft rustle of her robe dropping, hangers being banged back and forth as she sorted through her clothes and selected this item and that item, and then the soft sounds of clothes being pulled over smooth skin.

"Ta dah! You may look now."

He did.

"Well?" She was wearing comfortable jeans, a rugged looking shirt, and soft boots. Everything that she was wearing was brown, several shades of brown.

"Nice. A beautiful young woman."

She grunted at him. "Exactly how old are you

anyway?"

"Sometime, someday, I will tell you."

She sighed. "O.K., handsome hero who rescues damsels in distress, what do we do now?"

"Research."

"Research?"

"I am very good at that?"

"Good. I know a library that may be of some help. Shall we go? You drive, I will give directions."

And off they went.

Two people in a very small sporty car with the top down on a nice day for driving with the top down.

Chapter Four.

Research.

A Large Library In A Small Town.

She laughed as she looked at the structure. "It is very gothic. Makes a good setting for heros and damsels in distress. I use it as a setting in many of my novels." The building was dark stone with arched windows of many panes and a tower on either corner of the front and rear of the rectangular shape. "Of course, it isn't a library in my stories."

"Ummmm."

She parked and jumped out and waited for him to unfold from the passenger seat. He had decided that she ought to be the one driving.

They had turned from the main road into a very narrow lane transformed into a green tunnel by the thick planting of trees and shrubs that lined the way. One sharp turn some distance in and she slipped into a parking space next to the library.

He looked at the building and stretched. "Yes. It is a very good building for what we need to learn." He headed for the front entrance.

They walked up the wide stairs and through the double doors into a large open space with a high ceiling that disappeared into the gloom overhead.

An elderly gentleman appeared from somewhere, walked over and shook his hand. "Jonathon! Most welcome." And stared at her.

She was staring at him and Jonathon, mouth open. "Dee Grant," she hastily said.

Jonathon spoke very softly in one elderly ear.

The trio walked down the hall, around a corner, up a set of wooden stairs, down another but more narrow hall, and into a very large room filled with bookcases. As far as she could tell all the volumes in here were old, very old. She could smell the odor of leather bindings. And dust.

"Far end." The librarian pointed. "Start there." He spun away. "Call, if you need anything." And disappeared through a door and down the hall to somewhere.

"How did he know your name?"

"Ah ummm, I have been here before, um, looking things up."

She waved one hand. "Well then, lead on." She followed him down a narrow passage between the towering bookshelves into the dim light. The stacks seemed to stretch a long way.

Then, sooner that she thought, they stopped in an open space that had a table with two chairs.

He pointed at a shelf. "You start at his end. I will start over there."

"What are we looking for?"

"Information about your family. Anything that we can find about your family. Whatever is going on, it must have something to do with your family. There are pads of paper in those drawers, and pencils, and pens. Your real first name is unique, so see if you can spot that."

They started.

They finally met in the middle of a shelf, dust smudged, having filled page after page with notes.

"I am hungry," she said, making a neat stack of her pages of notes.

"Yes." He gathered his into a rough bundle and stood. "Let's."

He led her back and out and down and around, said goodbye to the librarian, and crammed himself in the passenger seat. When she was settled, he nodded. "At the bottom, turn right. There is a good restaurant not too far away."

As she turned right, she asked, "Come here often."

"Not for some time ago."

It was a Mexican restaurant. He dumped lots of salsa over everything.

"Obviously you like Mexican food,"

"Yes." He ordered another Margarita.

"Good thing that I am driving." She sipped her coffee, eyes scanning his face. This was either his fourth or fifth drink, but she couldn't detect any change. No slurring of what little conversation they had, no flush to his face, no fumbling with his knife or fork. Nothing.

He stood, waved over the waiter, and paid. "We will go to my house and see whether we have learned anything useful."

Chapter Five

Learning Useful.

A Small House Next To The Ocean.

"Dump everything on the table and lets see whether we can put everything we have noted into some logical chronological order."

They were in the living room. He dropped his bundle on the table and headed for the kitchen to start the coffee maker, waited, and then returned, cup in either hand. He handed her one.

"Well." He sipped. "Shall we see what we shall see?"

Dee sat and began to sort the pages into some sort of order. "How old were some of those volumes? I have never been in that section before."

"Old." He pushed his stack over to her. "Interleave these with those. Then we will start."

She did and leaned back. "I didn't realize that my family history stretched that far back. My folks never said anything like that. If fact, they never told me anything about my family at all. They were always going to." She stared at the papers seeing the rubble of her family home and the tendrils of smoke still rising.

"I will do it." He started with the first pages of notes and began to build a timeline. The day wandered into deep evening before he was finished. She watched how fast he worked. And nodded to herself, obviously he had done this sort of thing before.

He pushed back from the table and stood. "We can discuss all this in the morning." He pointed. "Use that bedroom. It is best that you stay here tonight." He looked into her eyes. "Just in case. Here you are safe."

She looked back. "From you?"

"From anything. I will be outside for some time. Good night." He spun and headed for the side door.

In the morning she found him in the kitchen, watching the sun come up, sipping coffee. He turned. "Morning." And handed her a filled cup.

"Early riser," she observed, and took a sip.

"Yes."

"I will make breakfast."

He nodded.

She made a large breakfast. "We skipped dinner."

When they finally returned to the table in the living room she saw that he had added a number of new pages of notes.

"Were you up all night?"

"No."

"Fast worker."

"Yes." He pointed at the top page. "Daliera occurs frequently among the first daughters in your family. Not all the first daughters, it tends to skip past generations at irregular intervals. It is an ancient name. In one of the books it dates to around 1060 or somewhere around that time. It could be much older, very much ancient. Very much long ago. The page was badly smudged in that volume."

She stared at the page. "I didn't find anything like that."

"Yes." He tapped the page. "The family name around then was Darthar, also a very old name, very long ago name. Two hundred years later they added Anathar, perhaps some marriage cross-tie. Then early 1320, plus or minus a bunch of years, it was changed to what you now know as d'Thonis a'Natur."

"Does that happen much?"

"Family changing names?"

"Uh huh."

"No. Not unless they were trying to hide for some reason. Ready?"

"For what?"

"Back to the library. We need to find where the names Darthar and Anathar will lead us. It is interesting."

She stood. "Sure. Let's go." And wondered why it was so interesting to him.

They stepped out into the darkness of early evening, holding pages and pages of additional notes.

He gently touched her shoulder, ever so gently. "You are in great danger, very great danger, Dee. I recognized one of the family names that your family had some sort of relationship with, long time ago. That family is to be worried about."

"Huh?"

"They tend to be not nice. I am beginning to think that perhaps one of them may be responsible for your visit from that Messenger thing."

He jerked and stuffed all his pages into her hands, grabbed her shoulders and spun her around to face him. "Close your eyes!"

"What?"

"DO IT!"

She did and felt his arms wrap around her and hold her tight. Well, she thought, that was sudden. He had gone from aloof to amorous with no transition at all. Then he let go and stepped back.

"You may open them now."

She gasped. They were standing in his living room.

"Better sit down. I will get some coffee." He walked toward the kitchen.

She dropped into a chair and dumped all their notes next to all their other pages of notes on the table nearby. Then she pinched her arm. It hurt.

"Here." He handed her a cup of coffee and sat.

She stared at him. "Now did you do that? It was you, wasn't it?"

He sipped. And nodded. "It is a skill. Ummmm, a minor skill."

She continued to stare at him, just stare. "Bull! That is not possible! People just can't do things like that!"

He nodded. "We are here."

She jumped to her feet. "I am going home!" And waved her hand wildly, sloshing coffee in all directions. "Forget all this, stuff! Forget that I asked you to do anything! Just forget it! My mind is getting buggered up and I think that you are responsible for that and I do not like it!" She spun and headed for the side door, stomping angrily away.

He blocked the door.

She ran for the kitchen door.

He blocked the way.

She hurtled through the living room and onto the deck.

He grabbed her by the back of her shirt before she could leap over the railing.

She screamed. And screamed. And screamed.

He waited, calm as calm ever was or could be. Then he gently pushed her into a chair in the living room and handed her a glass with a dark liquid in it. "Scotch."

She took a swallow, coughed, and rasped, "Can you, will you please explain, how or what?"

He sat in another chair. Not too close, not too far away, and took a sip. "Yes."

She shoved back in her chair and watched him very, very carefully. "Now?"

"Yes."

"How?"

He took another sip and looked at her. She looked calm enough. "This why I rarely agree to help one of the people, they do not want to understand. But! You came into my house and asked. So then, it became very hard for me to refuse. Especially when I could see great dark gathering around you and besides it is very difficult not to rescue a damsel in distress."

"And?" She took a careful sip this time. This scotch was powerful stuff.

"A character flaw, perhaps."

"And?" She took another careful sip.

"You are a beautiful young woman in very great danger."

"And?" She took another sip and relaxed, just a little bit. And didn't notice that he had refilled her glass.

"I come from a very old and ancient family. One of the not very many." He looked at her. "The people rarely understand, or care to understand, and have a bad habit of causing great problems, for us."

"The people?"

"Homo sapiens sapiens."

"Huh?"

"Ah um, what they think of as the humans, the

only humans. The people tend to be quite egocentric and to mix mythology and reality without knowing, or understanding, the difference. This most frequently results in them jumping to the very worst of conclusions which results in the very worst of results."

"And, you are?" She stared at him. He was beginning to sound just a little strange.

He stood and looked down at her. "In your eyes, that is, in the eyes of the people, in their usual and rather bizarre belief systems, I would not be considered human." He nodded. "Ah um, matter of viewpoint, so to speak. After all, we are a subspecies of Homo sapiens."

"What?" she whispered. "What are you talking about?" She was rapidly becoming convinced that she had somehow fallen in with a certifiable nut case of the worst sort. Or worse than that. If that was possible. She eyed the door.

He stepped closer. "Are you calm? Yet?"

She nodded. "Yes."

"No more screaming?"

"O.K."

"Ummmmm, no jumping up and running about the house?"

"Sure."

"You are positive about that?"

She nodded. Right now she would agree to anything, anything at all. And get out of here.

"Watch!" He stepped back and faded into black

shadow.

She blinked, and whispered all harsh whisper, "Jonathon?"

"Yes."

"Are you there?"

"Yes." He stepped from the darkness. "I am."

"Ahhhh?"

"A, ummmm, skill, a minor skill."

"Do you mind if I am totally confused as to whatever is happening?" Nobody does things like this guy was doing.

"No."

"Not human? You did say not human?" Her eyes scanned his face for something not human. He was just a very ordinary looking fellow.

"Yes. But it would be more accurate to say not Homo sapiens sapiens but Homo sapiens something else. A sub-species, as I said." He nodded. "We could, if we wished to do so, but don't, interbreed and raise fertile offspring. Well, the males could, but not the females. So we are close enough to them in that sense but, umm ah, different."

She nodded. "O.K., that makes sense, I suppose. So, what's the problem? The real problem? What's different?" She had never heard of a human sub-species, not in any of the books that she had read.

"Do you know of the author Bram Stoker?"

"Oh sure, he wrote Dracula." Everyone knew that book. Even if they hadn't read it.

"That is the person. It all stems from his mishmash of English sexual titillation, religious nonsense, and other cultural hangups of the time. And ever since then it has only gotten worse, ummm, in a manner of speaking."

She nodded. "Huh?" She wondered exactly how this conversation would be clinically evaluated. And what he was talking about. He hadn't sounded crazy, just very matter of fact. That could be a very bad sign, that casual belief.

"Heh heh heh," he intoned in his best Bella Lugosi tone of voice. "I do not drink . . . wine." Slowly he bent close and smiled at her, a very broad, very wide, teeth baring smile. His canines glittered in the soft light.

Her eyes flew open, round as round could get.

"A . . . vampire?" she whispered, pushing back into her chair, staring at those long, glistening fangs.

He stepped back. "We have been given that ignorant label. But it is all, mostly, nonsense." He stepped close, bent, reached out, gently took her hand and placed her fingertip at the pulse point on his wrist. "A beating heart."

He dropped into a chair. "And, as you have seen, I am not bothered by nor do I burst into flames in bright sunshine. I ate your Italian sausage with garlic. I eat lots of garlic and other members of that plant family. I use silver utensils in my house and my skin does not burn. Any kind of religious icon or symbol is not frightening.

And holy water is just plain old tap water." He waggled a loose hand at her. "O.K., Dee, you may now flee screaming into the night without being afraid that I will come swooping after you, gathering your luscious body in my talons, and biting you on the neck, transforming you into my willing slave and fellow blood sucker. By the way, it is a very nice neck." He licked his lips. And laughed, a soft, gentle laugh. He took a sip from his glass. "Scotch."

"Uh?"

"Yes?"

"How did you bring us here from there?"

"How do you run, ah, from here to there?"

"Ummm."

"Yes?"

"I, ah, just do."

"How do birds fly, fish swim, etc., etc.?"

"Ummmm."

"Yes?"

"And you can do lots of things, ah, like that?"

"Some. It is the way we are. It is the way I am." He nodded. "Perfectly normal. For us. For me."

"I feel like I fell down a different kind of rabbit hole."

"One way to look at it, I suppose. You still calm? Not frightened?" He watched her carefully.

She nodded, and realized that she was, fairly calm. "Yes. Strange. I feel like I should be very frightened. But I am not. I am calm, sort of." She stared at him. "Am I really safe? From you?"

"Safe as safe can be."

"You don't look all that different. Other than the canines. And a little pale."

"Yes."

"And how do I look to you?"

"A beautiful young woman." He nodded. "With a very bad problem."

"And you are going to help me with that?"

"Yes."

"Can you really help me?"

He laughed, a soft, gentle laugh. "Yes."

"How?"

"If I was a gypsy of the people I would tell you that you are going on a journey with a tall, handsome male, a long and dangerous journey of discovery and learning."

"Serious?"

"Maybe the handsome part was a stretch. But yes."

"Where are we journeying to?" She frowned.

"I do not know."

"Not very comforting a response."

"Best that I can do. Now."

"When?"

"We have already started, you and I."

She looked around at the very ordinary living room and a very ordinary looking house, and then back at him, a very ordinary appearing fellow, well, discounting long canines and pale skin. "We did?"

"Yes. You already know more about us than almost any of the people and we have begun to learn about your family. And others."

She nodded, stood, and looked down at him. "Right!" Then she frowned. "How come I do not feel strange about all this? Or scared? Or confused? Or something? Did you do something to me?" He better not have done something.

"I do not know for sure. No, that is not done, ah, mostly." He looked up at her through his eyebrows. "I think that it has to do with who you are, your family and all that. I think that is why you knocked on my door. There are other neighbors with doors to knock upon in the other direction. There is some very subtle process at work here which we will learn about, or perhaps discover, I think. It will be interesting, very interesting to discover." He pointed towards the hall. "You ought to sleep. In there."

She stepped back and looked at him. "You are not going to creep into my bedroom while I sleep and give me a little nip, are you?"

"No."

She laughed, kissed him on the forehead, spun away, and headed down the hall.

Oh well, he thought to himself, she seems to be a nice person, or whatever it is that she might be.

Chapter Six

More To Do.

A Small House Next To The Ocean.

She walked into the kitchen, large and light filled, and found him there, sunlight streaming through the window, doing something at the stove top. After filling a cup, she stepped over to see what he was doing.

"Scrambled eggs with cottage cheese and green chilies. Make some toast please."

She did and they ate breakfast. Over the last piece of toast, she asked, "How will I get my car back?"

"Go get it." He emptied his cup. "Ready?"

"For?"

"To go get your car."

"Sure."

He stood and held out his arms. "Step close. Close your eyes." She did and felt his arms envelope her.

"O.K., we are here. You have your keys, right?"

"Yep. Ah?"

"Ummmm?"

"Why did we do that?"

He waggled a hand at her car.

"Last night? Here?"

"There was something very not nice lurking in the dark."

"Oh. Get in."

He did. "Turn left."

And eventually he said, "Turn here. Park. Pack what you need, but very lightly please. Bare minimum of things. Please?"

He followed her into her house and into every room. "Just in case."

"Of?"

"Something not nice."

"Oh."

She straightened up from her packing and handed him a small gym bag. "Light enough?"

"Yes."

She watched his face. "You sure that we have to do this?"

"Yes."

"How are we going to get to where ever it is that we are going? My car?" She laughed softly. "Or by Air Jonathon?"

Well, he thought to himself, she does have a nice laugh. "Car. I will give directions. You will drive. More research. Different library."

As they crested the ridge, he asked, "Do you have house insurance?"

"Of course. Why?"

"It just blew up."

"What?" The car skidded to a halt. She jumped out and ran back up to the top of the grade and stared at the column of black smoke in the distance. "My house? That is my house?"

"Yes." He stood by her side. "We should be on our way."

She sat on the shoulder of the road and looked up, eyes glistening, tears running down her cheeks. "That was me, that house. All my writings, all my books, all my everything."

He stood, calm as calm, and waited, until she was done and had heaved herself to her feet.

"Tell me that it will all turn out all right."

"Can't do that."

"Not very comforting. You could lie."

"Ummmm."

She plopped into the driver's seat and watched him sit and fasten his seat belt. "You know," she said, "I think that I could kill whoever is responsible for doing that."

He sighed, a soft, gentle sigh. "Turn left at the first intersection."

The sun was setting when they parked at their destination.

"Wow, super modern. I was expecting another gothic building." It was a great square, all large windows and glistening metallic blue covering.

"Ummm."

As they exited their car, one of the glass doors swung wide and a young woman came bounding down the stairs to them. "Jonathon." She wrapped her arms around him in a great hug.

"Ooof!"

Releasing him, she beamed at the woman standing next to him. "I am Karanly. Who are you?"

"Dee Grant."

"The author? My goodness, I read every one of your books." She shook Dee's hand. "Come in, come in. I am sure that you two have much to do. Jonathon never comes here unless he is researching something in the archives."

Dee followed them inside and down the stairs, deep into the archives.

"I am the librarian today," stated Karanly. "What are you looking for this time?"

He explained.

"That old, that old. Well, I think that I know exactly the collection that you need to pour through. This way."

The trio walked deeper and deeper into what seemed to Dee to be an ever expanding basement.

Karanly unlocked a large wooden door, shoved it in, pushed past it, and snapped on a number of lights.

"Call if you require anything. I would suggest that you start with that shelf." She pointed, spun, kissed Jonathon on the cheek, and hummed away into the darkness of the basement.

So they did. They started with that shelf.

Many volumes later, they finished.

Karanly came down between two tall bookshelves and looked at them. "Ah, well satisfied. Follow me." She led them to the end of the bookcase and through a door, then up the stairs, and in what felt to Dee to be a very short distance, out onto the main floor.

"This way. Here should do." The room they entered was not too small, not too large, furnished with a table littered with pads of paper, pens and pencils. Two large comfortable looking chairs were set by the table. Karanly slipped silently out the door.

Jonathon stood by one of the chairs, dropped his many pages of notes on the table top, and nodded to Dee. "When we finish merging these notes with our others we ought to know very much of what we ought to know."

He dumped all their previous notes, charts, and annotated pages next to the first pile. "I brought everything." And nodded at her.

Dee nodded back and smiled. "A small skill."

"Yes."

He sat and began to work.

Karanly bounced into the room. "Time to eat." And beckoned them from the room. They had just finished. "We can discuss everything afterwards."

Down a hall, through a door into a room where

dinner was waiting.

As they ate Dee puzzled over the strange behavior of this librarian. She seemed to always know what they were doing. Then she wondered about the other librarian. She thought it might make the framework for an interesting novel. Maybe even two.

The food was good, the wine even better. Suddenly she realized that Karanly was biting into a rather large turkey drumstick with rather long canines.

Karanly looked across the table and winked at her.

After dessert, vanilla ice cream with sliced strawberries, Dee and Jonathon and Karanly returned to the paper strewn table to discuss what they knew. There were now three chairs set by that table.

"So," said Karanly, looking at Jonathon as they sat.

He shoved a chart at her and tapped one portion of it.

"Ummmmm." Karanly rapidly scanned the rest of it. She glanced up at Dee and stared.

"Yes." He nodded. And explained to Dee. "It is a long and very ancient family tree. They were somewhere in the mountainous region of eastern Europe and have had associations with these two families." He pushed two more charts over to Karanly.

When she finished looking them over, he carefully slid another chart over and set it on top of the others. "This is the problem."

Karanly looked at it and hissed, "Them!"

"Yes."

"What?" asked Dee.

"A very not nice family," grumbled Karanly.

Then she smiled at Dee. "You have a very interesting family. Very."

"Oh?"

"Yes." Jonathon gathered up all the pages into a neat stack. "A good start."

"Start?"

"Yes." He stood. "Now we must visit and, ah um, talk with some, um, individuals."

Karanly grinned at her and nodded at Jonathon. "It is like that strange insurance company says, you are in good hands." She stood, walked around and kissed him on the cheek. "Do be wise careful, brother."

Then she walked over and kissed Dee on the forehead. "Yum, yum." She laughed and left the room.

"She jokes." He stood.

"Brother?"

"Yes." He stepped back and beckoned. "Step close."

She did. "And close my eyes."

"Yes." Ah well, he thought, maybe she will be able to understand what they had been discussing. He wrapped his arms tightly around her. It was interesting.

Chapter Seven

Interesting Folk To Visit.

A Very Large Place.

Releasing her, he stepped back and turned her around. Here it was day not night.

"A castle?" Dee stared at it. It was a large black stone, gloomy looking castle with pediments and towers all along the upper walls.

"Yes. Hongor lives here. He knows much about many of the families. It is his hobby of a sort. Oh, and don't be surprised. Please?"

"Sure." She nodded and wondered, now what? Everything had been surprising so far. How could it not be? And why that warning now?

Jonathon stepped up to the door and pushed it open. It was a small door built into a very large door. "May we visit?"

"Jonathon," rumbled the large and thick in every direction man that stood looking at them. "Do come in. Both."

Hongor lumbered off and through a large archway. "This way." And then into a room and dropped into a large chair, one of many that were set around the table. "What?"

"Have you heard of this family." Jonathon told him the name.

"Ah mah," rumbled Hongor. "That one. Yes. A very quiet family." He nodded.

"Do you know where they live?"

"No. But their dwelling is that way." He jabbed one thick finger vaguely at one wall. "Two mountain ranges over, maybe more. Not far."

"Nobody lives there?"

"No. They left not many long ago."

Dee squinted at Hongor. And wondered at such a strange way to describe the passage of time, or direction.

"Is this, um, dwelling still intact?"

Hongor nodded.

"And this family?" Jonathon spoke the name.

"Close link with that quiet family. But they are no more. The last one didn't get past 1400 or 1500, around that time."

"And this family?" Jonathon spoke the name.

Hongor nodded. "There are still some, or one, I think. They dwell over there." A thick hand and arm waggled at a different wall.

"Near?"

"Not far. Two or three countries over."

Dee marveled at the strange way Hongor treated distance. Again. A very strange way of talking.

"And this family?" Jonathon spoke the name.

Hongor hissed and lurched upright.

Dee stared at him. It seemed to her that Hongor was getting vague around the edges. Then she jerked back in her chair.

Bright yellow eyes peered at her over a long muzzle, bright white canines poked down past the lower jaw. "A very not nice family. Twisted, bent strange. Do not visit that ugly. They are ill mannered."

"Thank you, Hongor." Jonathon stood.

"Pleasure, Jonathon," said Hongor, now looking like himself. "And you also, beautiful young woman." He licked his lips as she stood.

Outside the door, he turned to face her. "Frightened?"

She nodded. "Some. It was a surprise."

"Hongor is a friend. And well behaved, mostly."

"Mostly?"

"Step close."

She did. "And close my eyes." She did, leaned against him, cheek against his chest, and threw her arms around him.

He wrapped his arms around her. Ah well, he thought.

A cool breeze ruffled past them.

"Open your eyes and turn around," he said.

"WOW!"

They stood halfway up the flank of a mountain, one of many in a long chain. The top of this one had gathered a few clouds and a permanent snow cover. The meadow where they stood stretched upwards from them in a gentle slope to the base of the structure towering above them. It was half chateau, half fairytale castle. Everything was constructed of light red wood perched on heavy dark green stone foundation walls. The whole thing stretched along the slope rather than up and down the mountain's flank..

She stared here and there and looked up at the many storied building. "Who lives here?"

"No one, ummmm, mostly."

"This place is empty? Mostly?" She stared at him and wondered how such a large building could be empty, mostly.

"Yes."

"Really?" She looked back at it.

"Yes. This is your house."

She jerked around and stared at him. "Mine?" And laughed.

She spun back around to take another look at the great structure, and then turned back and frowned at him. "Joke, right?"

"No. So far we have found no record of any living relative of your's or any siblings. It appears that you are the last living member of your lineage. Do you have any children?"

Dee laughed. "No!"

"No males panting around wanting to fertilize you?"

"Oh that!" She shrugged. "Well, anyone who is even a little well known and is female has those kinds of guys turning up."

"Perhaps you ought to let one. Then chase him away. An offspring would insure the next generation."

"Pretty casual."

"Shall we go in?"

"Can I?

"All your's"

She laughed, then started up the slope, and up the long stairs to the only door that she could see. They stopped in front of it. Dee was breathing heavily. He wasn't.

"High altitude," he said. He indicated the door. "You go first. You should be allowed to go inside."

Dee frowned, nodded and pushed. The door opened quietly and swung in and wide. She stepped inside. "Wow! Again." She spun around. "Amazing to say the least."

He nodded, stepped close, and rapped one knuckle on something hard in the opening that neither of them could see. "Ah!"

"What?"

"Invite me in, please?"

"Oh! Jonathon, do come in."

He stepped inside and looked up and down the long hall with the large windows looking out at the meadow. "Nice place." It had been a long time.

They started walking along the hall.

"How does one person live in something like this?" Dee waggled her arm at their surroundings.

"You could have servants. Invite friends to visit."

She stopped and looked out a window. "There are no roads out there. How can anyone come to visit? I don't have any friends. Oh, sorry. Didn't mean you."

"Ummm." He looked up and down the hall. "Wonder where the library is? We need to find information for you on your lineage."

She pointed down the hall at a door. "Through there." She took one step in that direction, stopped, and gasped, turned and stared at him. "How did I know that?" She blinked. "Now I am frightened."

"Ummmm." He walked up to the door. "Shall we open it?"

She nodded.

They walked into the library.

She spun and grabbed him. "Hold me. Please?"

He did.

"Strange, strange, strange, strange," she mumbled against his chest. "Strange, strange, strange, strange."

He waited. Calm as calm.

She sighed, sucked in a deep breath, and stepped back, eyes glistening wet. "I need a vacation. From this sort of stuff. And what do you mean, my lineage?" She wiped her eyes on her sleeve.

He reached out and tilted up her chin with one finger. "Ummmm. You cannot do that, take a vacation.

You are not safe. Unless you wish to live here. Here you will be very safe." He bent and kissed her forehead. "Let us look for a book that will tell us something about those other families and your lineage. There should be some records somewhere in here. You need to know."

"O.K."

Finally, part way down the third shelf in the fifth section, they found it. It was labeled: *Family Linkages.*

Sitting at the table, shoulder touching shoulder, Dee opened the book and began to slowly turn the thick pages as they began to search. Many pages later, he pointed.

"There. You have a cousin."

By the last page they found her parents listed and their only daughter.

"Hungry?"

"Yes."

Karanly popped through the door. "Next room over. Nice place, Dee."

They followed her to the correct room and sat at the table set for three, the top covered with platters and bowls of steaming food.

"I won't ask," she mumbled as she took some more from one of the bowls. How did his sister do this?

Over dessert, Karanly smiled at Dee. "So, you met Hongor. Did he behave?"

"Mostly." Dee looked from one to the other and yawned. "I am really tired. I need to sleep."

Karanly bounded to her feet. "Know your way?"

Dee yawned again and nodded. "Strange as it is, I do." She walked from the room and down the hall and up the correct staircase to her bedroom. She thought that she must have lived here when she was little. And wondered what her lineage, as Jonathon had phrased it, really was all about. How could this huge place be her's? Her parents had certainly never talked about something like this.

As she looked around the room she wondered who took care of the place. There was no dust, everything was clean and neat. And who had set that table and prepared all that food? She certainly hadn't heard anyone else. And she didn't remember a kitchen being somewhere either. At least from what she thought that she remembered.

She shrugged and then took a long, hot soak in a gigantic tub and finally crashed into the large bed, sound asleep in moments.

In the morning, rested, and feeling pretty good, Dee stopped Jonathon. "Who is taking care of this place?"

"Ummmmm?"

"It is clean, neat, and tidy, and doesn't look abandoned. My bedroom was fresh and neat, ready to occupy. Just like a motel, or hotel. Soooo, who is doing all this? Why haven't I seen a soul, anywhere. And I haven't heard anyone either."

"It is the house.

"Huh?"

"The house does it."

"This place is automated?" She looked around, searching for outlets, slots in the walls, places for robots to pop from or to scurry into.

"In a manner of speaking."

"Ah, one more thing? Manner of speaking?"

"Yes."

"How come this great structure hasn't been seen? Broken into? Vandalized? Seen by satellites and all that, airplanes?"

"Ah, ummmm. It is a universal house skill. Being there but not being there. Unless the house is in a town, the people and their things can not see it. So far."

"What about accidently bumping into it? Bumping into something unseen?"

"Ummmm ah. It is the house, um, protection. The people just go around, never toward. They just always do and are never aware of doing that."

"Ever stranger," mumbled Dee.

Karanly bounded from a nearby door. "Breakfast is served." She smiled at Dee. "It is the house sprites."

"The what?"

"They do it. Neat and tidy, and all the other things."

Dee stared at her. "House sprites? There are little things whizzing around doing things all over the place?"

Karanly nodded. "Not all are small." And

popped back through the door and back out again holding a cup of coffee. "Watch." She dumped it on the floor. "Come in." She held the door open.

The door closed behind them.

Karanly opened the door and pointed at the floor. It was clean. "See?"

Dee dropped heavily into a chair and mumbled, "Alice In Wonderland. Sorta."

Karanly served breakfast. Dee's eyes jumped from place to place searching for sprites.

"Might as well stop," said Karanly. "It takes a special call. Family specific."

Dee mumbled around her toast. "Boy, did my parents ever do a lousy job of educating me."

Karanly looked at her brother and nodded.

He sat still as ever and didn't say anything.

Dee ate some of the scrambled eggs and mumbled, mostly to herself, "Vampires who aren't, guys that look like over-sized dogs and aren't, house sprites. Strange, strange, strange, strange."

Karanly frowned at Jonathon.

Dee's head snapped up. "What?" She had been watching a crumb on the table cloth, waiting for it to disappear.

Then she glared at Karanly. "How did you get in?" She jabbed a finger at Jonathon, who ducked. "I had to invite him."

Karanly smiled. "Family."

"You gonna pop in and out while we are gone?"

"Can't. You have to be at home and to have invited us in."

"Every time?"

Karanly nodded.

"Oh." Dee looked down. The crumb was gone. "Damn sneaky," she grumbled.

"When you leave, we have to leave," said Karanly.

"Really?"

"Yes," said Jonathon.

"You could give us permission to stay." Karanly grinned at her. "When you are gone."

Dee sighed. "Is any of this stuff written down somewhere, like in an instruction manual?"

Karanly looked doubtful.

Jonathon stood. "We have to go."

So did Dee. "Who?"

"Distant relatives."

"Oh." She looked at Karanly. "Do you wish to stay?"

"No."

"O.K." She walked over to Jonathon, leaned against him, her cheek against his chest, closed her eyes, and wrapped herself around him. "Let's go."

Karanly stared at him.

He shrugged. And they were gone. All three of them.

The house sprites made the place neat and tidy.

They stood and looked at the building. It stood at the edge of a very dense forest not too far from a small village. The structure was quite modest, at least as compared to everything that Dee had seen so far. It looked like a rather small cottage constructed of wood with a light brown thatched roof.

"Who lives here?"

"A distant cousin. Many times removed, of your's.

Dee sucked in a deep breath, stepped up to the door, exhaled, and gently knocked. "A cousin," she mumbled to herself.

The door flew open, a young man stood there, stared at her, eyes flying wide, and screamed. The door slammed shut.

She stared at Jonathon. "I didn't do anything, did I?" And thought, pretty strange cousin.

"No."

"Then?"

"Try again. Say something."

Dee shoved the door open and before anything could happen shouted into the interior, "HELLO!"

He staggered sideways and crashed to lean against the wall. "Hello," he whispered.

Jonathon leaned closed to Dee and said softly, "Use your real name. Introduce yourself. Your first name."

"Oh." Dee looked at the young man who was watching her ever so carefully. "Hi. My name is Daliera.

Who might you be?"

He straightened up, walked over, and touched her shoulder with a very careful fingertip. "Solid." He nodded to her. "I am Kraz d'Anathar. An uncle, many, many back, four times removed, married a niece of your's, three removed. I though you to be dead and a ghost." He touched her again, just to be sure.

"Why would you think that I am dead?"

"Your durta abode was swallowed in fire."

She looked at Jonathon. "My house?"

"A small unguarded secondary or tertiary residence of little regard. The people house that you left."

"Oh, we weren't there," she said to Kraz. "This is Jonathon, a, ummm, friend. Jonathon Harkerness."

Kraz frowned at him.

Jonathon said something swift.

Kraz bowed. "Welcome . . . Jonathon." He looked at them. "Do come in, both." And led them into a room for sitting and talking.

"Most kind," said Jonathon.

"Yah," said Dee. "Most kind." She looked around, thinking that maybe here the sprites would be more visible.

"So," said Kraz, after much throat clearing, "why come you here?"

Jonathon explained. Kraz sucked in his breath. "That is a very not nice family." He shook his head. "Little help can I offer. I am the last." He smiled warmly at Dee. "Would you like to mate?"

Dee surged to her feet. "NO!"

Kraz looked dejected. "You don't have any sisters, do you?"

"No." She dropped into her chair. "Sorry. You surprised me. Wasn't ready for a marriage proposal."

Kraz shook his head.

"Huh?"

"Just mate."

"Strange," she mumbled. Everything always was strange.

Kraz looked puzzled at Jonathon.

He just sat. Calm as calm.

Kraz stood."I will bring the family book." And hurried from the room. The door slammed shut.

In a moment or two, he was back dropping a large, thick, and heavy tome on the table. He opened it to the very last pages. "Special section." And spun the book around so that they could read it.

"Ta'Qarna Farthan." Jonathon looked up at Kraz. "Know where their house is?"

"Hidden. Dark hidden."

"That their true name?"

"Most true. A special secret knowledge."

"Much debt, Kraz."

Karanly popped through the door, smiled at her brother, and grinned at Kraz. "Yum."

He jerked back.

"First sister," said Jonathon.

She yanked a chair over and sat next to Kraz, her chair banging into his, patted his thigh, looked at him, and licked her lips.

He stared at her.

She leaned across and kissed his cheek. "Oh, boy." And did it again. "Do you like librarians? I like luscious young males."

Jonathon stood. "We must go."

Dee stood and followed him into the hall.

"Bye, Dee, first brother," called Karanly gaily as the door slammed shut behind them.

"Shhhhh," said Jonathon as he wrapped her in his arms.

They went to her house and spent four days resting. He thought that it would be good for her. Let her relax and get used to things.

Then, off they went again.

The structure was low to the ground and appeared to be a large square shape.

"Library," said Jonathon. "Very special library."

Something large, something dark fell upon them, grabbing for Dee as Jonathon shoved her away, flying through the air to tumble and roll in the thick grass.

Dee sat up and stared. Something grey with great wings, claws, and fangs was ripping, tearing, and scattering bits and pieces of a great ugly black something, that was snarling, growling, and rapidly changing shape.

Grass, soil, and other things flew in all directions as the monsters struggled and fought. Then the grey one stepped from the carnage and walked in her direction. She leaped to her feet, spun, and ran. For two steps.

A great hand clamped over her shoulder, covering the side of her neck and the shoulder, and held her in place. She screamed.

"Shhhhh," said the monster. "You are safe." And released her.

She ran and banged on the door. "OPEN UP IN THERE! LET ME IN!"

"Not by the hair of my chinny chin chin."

She stared at the door. "What?"

"Open," said Jonathon, stepping to her side.

The door swung in.

A tall man stood there. "I am the librarian."

"Certainly don't look like one of The Three Little Pigs." She spun around and looked out at the meadow and the mess. "Where did that thing go?"

"The Dark Finder died," said Jonathon.

"And what is that?"

"I will explain. Later."

"Welcome," said the librarian. "Do come in."

"Really dumb joke," grumbled Dee as she pushed past the librarian. She rubbed her shoulder. "What is going on?"

"Shhhh," said Jonathon.

She turned and stared at him, silently mouthing, "You?"

"I will explain. Later." He handed the librarian a slip of paper. "This family."

The librarian looked, read it, and jerked. "Many layers below."

Jonathon nodded.

They stood in a low ceiling cavern of rock with weak illumination from small lamps.

"This way." The librarian walked off.

And, a short time later, or maybe a long time later, they arrived. Dee wasn't really sure how long they had been walking.

A single, very large, very thick, bound in red leather, book sat on the high table by itself.

The librarian pointed. "Everything known and much guessed about that family is written there. I will leave you now. Do be cautious and careful. Hate to loose visitors, we get so few these days." He turned and disappeared into the gloom.

"Ummmmm." Jonathon dragged a thick pad and writing instruments from a drawer in the table and set them on the table. "I will read, you will take notes."

Dee cleared her throat. "O.K."

They started. He read very rapidly what she was to write down.

Outside, high above where they stood, reading and taking notes, things snarled and growled and battered at the door and windows and walls of the library. Monsters with great wings and curved talons tore at the roof.

The library was guarded many, many layers deep. The assault went on and on and on.

The librarian sat at a small table and sipped tea and ate scones.

Through the small window he watched the turmoil outside.

And marveled at someone's lack of self-control.

"Done," said Jonathon, snapping the book closed.

Dee gathered up all the pages of notes. They had hurried so fast that she had no idea what she had written. Jonathon had rattled out the sentences so fast she could barely keep up much less pay attention to their meaning.

"This way," said the librarian, stepping from the gloom.

Upstairs, on the main floor, standing in the main hall, the librarian looked at them. "Be there else you wish?"

"No," said Jonathon.

"Nope," agreed Dee.

The librarian pointed at the floor. "Leave from this spot. It is getting crowded outside." He sat at his table and refilled his tea cup and watched the mess beyond his window. And shook his head.

In their usual way, Jonathon and Dee left.

"My house?" asked Dee.

"Inside. Quickly."

She threw open the door, jumped inside, spun and said, "Do come in, Jonathon."

He did. The door closed.

"Dinner is ready," called Karanly from an open door not far down the hall.

"How does she do that?"

"Fast traveler."

"Well," gurgled Karanly as she served the food. "If his son can get a mate from one of the other families that family should be good for some time."

After dinner, they retired to a more comfortable room to sit and relax.

Dee looked at him. "O.K., explain."

He looked at Karanly.

"Relax, brother."

He nodded. "It was me."

"Ahhhhh?" Dee shook her head.

He stood. Ah well, he thought to himself, it was bound to happen. He shifted and changed and altered until his head almost touched the high ceiling.

The deep voice whispered to her, "Don't panic, Dee. It is just me."

Karanly watched Dee carefully. After all, they were in her house. Even if she didn't know much about anything, she might accidently do something dangerous to them.

Dee nodded and cleared her throat. "O.K., back to normal or whatever that was."

He altered and shifted and changed until he was just Jonathon again. "That is why we have so little to do with the people as possible. In that form we look like the devil that they often believe in, the one they love to hate, ummmmm, depending, ah ummm, of course, upon the strength of their superstitious belief, ah, that is. And the variety."

Karanly laughed. "In the not too long ago, we used to go around in our costume, so to speak, and get lots of candy during their Halloween celebration. People laughed and thought that we were cute. We stayed small. Just for that." She shook her head. "But we don't do that anymore."

Jonathon stood. "Going upstairs to think." And left them to themselves.

Karanly thumbed through their latest collection of notes. "I think that not nice one has come unhinged for some reason. He is up to no good. He wants your body for a not nice purpose." She stood. "Do not go anywhere until I get back. It is time to talk with a distant cousin. Bye." She stepped into the hall and was gone.

Dee began to read the notes so carefully taken in such a rush that nothing she wrote she had actually paid attention to. Then she jumped up, ran down the hall, turned into the appropriate room, and lost her last meal into the appropriate fixture. That family was really, ah, not nice.

She wiped her face with a handy towel, washed it, sloshed water around in her mouth and spit. Then she decided to walk around some, just to see what this place was like. Just to think about something else.

Out the door and down the hall she wandered, looking out the many windows that lined this hall, and wondered how anyone could live in such an immense structure by themselves. Then she thought she ought to get some roller skates. So far, none of the information that they had gathered had suggested that she came from a family large enough to need a place like this. So, she wondered, why did anyone have such a large and sprawling place to live in?

Far down the hall she could see light spilling from an open door. It was the first open door that she had seen so far. So she walked that way.

She stepped inside and stopped. "Wow!"

This room looked the throne rooms seen in every costume drama set in the era of knights that Hollywood had ever made. Opposite the door, next to the far wall was a raised platform upon which sat, she supposed, the throne. It was a rather plain wooden chair with a cushion seat and a high padded back and arm rests. She smiled and thought, all this place needs is lots of folk standing around in fancy clothes and large guards dressed in heavy armor holding great swords. The ceiling was arched, the walls all ornate wood paneling.

She walked down the central path, lighter stone than the rest of the floor, up the steps and sat down, and laughed. She did feel rather regal sitting up here looking down at the empty throne room which it certainly might be. She wondered what period of time it had been when some of her family had lived here and had some sort of royalty running about.

She leaned back in the chair. It was quite comfortable. And sighed.

"What is your wish, Princess?" asked a soft and gentle voice.

She jumped to her feet. "WHAT?" There was no one there. That she could see. "Who spoke? Is this one of the sprites?"

"Oh, dear," sighed the voice. "Have I offended you in some manner unknown?"

Dee spun around and around. "O.K. smart guy, show yourself! This in not funny!"

"I," stated the voice with gathering dignity, "am neither a jester nor other folk of that ilk." The light shimmered to one side of the throne and became a rather short something.

The person, or something, was dressed in clothes of various shades of blue that went well with the rather soft blue of his skin. He bowed. "Princess?" And waved one hand of rather long fingers at the throne. "Do seat yourself so you may converse in comfort."

She sat. "Come around in front so I can see you."

"Of course."

"So, who, or what, are you?"

"I am Ar'ga'da'fazza'din'ban'ahm'na. You may address me, if you wish, as Ar."

She nodded. "O.K., Ar, what do you do?"

"I am your personal Advisor, the one who answers questions, provides Advice and Wise Council, and sees to it that your every wish, agah, with the usual allowances, of course, may come to be." He sighed. "It has been some long time since last you were here. Your parents left when you were much smaller. It has been ever so silent here ever since. Quite boring, if I may say so."

Dee sighed. "Just getting ever stranger," she mumbled. "Why did you call me Princess?"

Ar's mouth flew open, then snapped shut. "Why because that is what you are. You are a Princess from a long line of Princesses of this noble house, ahem, ahem, the most noble lineage of all the families still extent among the Feyra."

"Feyra?"

"Indeed."

"Who are?"

He stared at her. "Oh, my, dear, dear, dear. Your parents were most negligent. The Feyra are us. The Other Folk. The unseen dwellers who tend to not interact with the people who swarm everywhere."

She slumped and stared at him. "Me? I am one of, um, the Feya? Is that is what Jonathon meant about him being a sub-species?"

He frowned at her. A Princess did not slump on the throne. "Most true. Ahem, ahem, if I might point out your, ummmmm, posture?"

"Sure. What?"

"A Princess just does not slump when sitting on the throne!"

Dee jerked upright.

Ar smiled, rows of sharp teeth. And bowed to her.

She stood and headed for the door out. "Come on, Ar, I am exploring this place. You can be my guide."

He trotted to her side. "My pleasure, Princess."

A number of hours later, the pair were following a twisting corridor in the upper reaches of the place.

Dee nodded her head at their surroundings. "This place is amazing. Really and truly amazing."

Ar smiled. "It was built and added to over many a long time ago." He cleared his throat as they stepped into a great open space that had numbers of deep, rock-lined rooms in all the walls.

"Ahem, Princess?"

"Yes."

"I am your Advisor and Councilor."

"Uh huh."

"Then I must caution you. You guests, are, ummmm . . . "

"What?"

"It is not good that they know your true name

but do not share their's with you."

"True name?"

"To know a true name is to gain a, ah, um, certain access otherwise impossible to get. It is a, um, deeply personal thing to do."

"Do you know where he is?"

"Of course. Shall I bring him to your presence?"

She smiled. "Let's do it."

She blinked. "Hello, Jonathon."

He looked at Ar. "Ah, I see. You are learning."

"I am certainly doing that all right."

"Ummmmm."

"O.K., spill it! What is your true name?"

He stared at her.

"Ar told me all about that!" she snapped.

He sighed, a soft, gentle sigh.

"Fair is fair," she growled. "You know mine, tell me your's."

He straightened up and bowed deeply. "Of course, Princess. My true name is Othara a'Anathar a'Mdator a'Zguar a'Winfa a'Apatin a'Relda d'Darthar." He smiled at her, a soft, gentle smile. And bowed again. "I am Othara, Lord of both branches of the family Darthar and Head of House Darthar. And now we are well met, Princess Daliera."

"Ar?" She turned.

"The most powerful house of all the houses, Princess. And long ago and far away linked to your family in the very earliest of times almost before memory."

Her head snapped around, she glared at him. "You knew this all along?"

"No. But I was beginning to suspect. From our research."

"So, do I call you Lord and bow and scrape?"

Ar sucked in a deep breath.

"No. I prefer Jonathon for this time, Princess. May I still address you as Dee?"

"Sure."

"Why are you up here, Dee?"

"Exploring. Ar is telling me all about this place."

"Ummm."

She popped in, smiling broadly. "Hi, Princess." And made a deep bow and looked up through her eyebrows at Dee, and said, "Everyone bows." She straightened up. "I am Karanalador. Just tack on all the rest. So I am Karanalador blah blah blah. But I use Karanly."

She stepped over and threw an arm around Dee's shoulders. And kissed her on the cheek. "So how are you doing, Princess?"

"Head's spinning. Hard to believe. Hard to live. I know so little about so much." She smiled. "But I found Ar in the throne room, so I am learning about all kinds of things." She whispered in a close ear, "Do you have any idea why my parents did what they did?"

"No. I don't think that they told anyone why they fled into obscurity.

"Fled?"

"Seemed like it."

Karanly stopped walking. "May I go get something to eat. I am still very hungry. With your permission, of course."

"Sure," said Dee to empty space. She waved a hand. "What are those stone rooms for?"

Ar pointed. "Those?"

"Yes."

"They are the nests of the family house beasts."

"So where are they?"

"In the forests, all about. They were released when your parents left. Shall I call them in?"

"Are they friendly?"

"Of course. To members of the family and invited guests."

"Sure."

Openings appeared in several of the walls. Sunlight streamed in and a soft breeze tickled past them. Something thumped in and clumped heavily over to one of the alcoves, rumbling loudly.

Dee stared at it, then at Ar. "What is that?"

"This is Gooda. You named him that when you were both very little."

"But, what is it?"

"It is a Kartar."

It grumbled at her. The thing appeared to be shaped, more or less, like an extremely large grizzly bear but it was covered in thick, light green scales that shimmered in the light. Great canines protruded down over the lower jaw.

"I was expecting dogs."

"Oh," said Ar. "The Hounds will be here soon."

"Perhaps," suggested Jonathon, "we could be somewhere else for awhile?"

Ar pointed down. "One of the rooms with a view. One might visit there, have something to eat?"

"Good idea." Dee started that way. "Thanks, Ar."

"Oh, my," gasped Ar.

"What?" asked Dee. "Now?"

"I have never been thanked before."

"Really?"

"Not done, Princess."

"Small change, Ar, small change." She pushed the door and walked out.

They were in a comfortable room just off the downstairs hall. They sat at the table set against the wall directly under the large window. Things seemed to be moving inside the dimness of the forest.

Karanly munched on something that crunched loudly.

By the time they had finished their meal, soft grumbling was coming through their door.

Ar leaned close. "The hounds are here, Princess."

Karanly bounced to her feet. "Let's see them."

Dee jumped up and headed for the door, Ar by

her side. "Ahh, maybe I ought to go first?" said Dee.

"Yes," said Jonathon as Dee pulled the door open.

"Those are dogs?" Dee stared at the four large things, the large horse-sized things, vaguely dog-like in appearance.

"Hounds," corrected Ar.

The four crowded close and stared into Dee's face. The hound shoulders were taller than the top of her head.

"Pretty big," she mumbled. "What are they?"

"A rare breed, Princess," said Ar.

"And?" She reached out and stroked a long muzzle. "Soft fur." The hounds were a light red brown color. She sniffed. They smelled like scorched wood, and smoke.

"The proper name for the breed is Inferno Hound."

A long tongue slithered out and over her hand. Then warm breath caressed it.

"They are nice, ah, for very large." She turned. "I am going to see what else there is." She turned and pointed. "Let's go that way, Ar. See you later, puppies."

Pushing the door aside, she headed down the hall, then turned, and called, "Oh, all right, come on, you guys."

The four hounds crowded after her and jostled each other as they came.

"Take it easy, you mutts. There is no hurry."

Ar stared, wide goggle eyes, at her. "Princess!"

"What?" Sharp talons clattered on the stone floor behind her as she walked.

"Ah," said Ar. "Umm, nothing." This Princess was certainly different than any of the other ones that he had served in this family in a very long career. Really different.

And so the day progressed.

Dee wandered the halls accompanied by Ar who ran a constant commentary on anything and everything they saw. The hounds clattered along behind them seeming to enjoy a freedom, apparently denied the other house beasts who were assembling, slowly, in the House Beast quarters.

Karanly and Jonathon popped in and out doing whatever they were about. They were waiting on Dee.

"Ar?" asked Dee. "Do the house beasts only guard the house? Is that why they are called House Beast?"

"Oh no," gasped Ar. "They are called House Beasts because they belong to The House, ah umm oh, house being merely another term for family. So, I suppose, if you wish, you could call them Family Beasts."

"Oh." Dee nodded. "So then, they are my beasts as I appear to be the only family that there is."

Ar nodded. "Just so, Princess." She had tried, unsuccessfully, to keep him from calling her Princess all the time, and had finally decided it was a habit that he couldn't break.

"Sooooo," said Dee, causing a small bit of alarm for Ar. "If I wanted to, they could travel with me?"

"Ammmm dak zummmmm," mumbled Ar.

"What?" She stared at him. He was shimmering, pale, and back again. "Are you sick?"

"I am never sick!" He bowed deeply. "Pardon, Princess." He sucked in a deep breath. "You shouldn't do that, errr, travel with them."

"Why not?"

"The people would scream and yell and run every which way and then try to do awful things to them. It really wouldn't do, not at all."

"Ummm," she said.

Ar sighed. "Princess, you are slowly learning ever so much about your family and the other families of the Feyra." One quivering finger pointed at a window. "But those people, beings, out there can't seem to accept to us, not even a teeny, tiny bit." He shrugged. "Well, every once in awhile, one of them here, one of them there, do, but it is rare, very, very rare. So, one has to be careful out there, very, very careful. Can't have people riots, can we? Can't start another of those witch hunt things, can we? Not . . . at . . . all." He sighed even more deeply. "Your life is going to be hard enough as it is, being who you are and all."

Dee stopped walking, turned, and looked at him, and said, "Normal fangs. I seen to have these, ah, normal fangs." She curled her lip to display her canines.

"Ah, that."

"Yesssssss?"

"The families vary in, ummm, many of their attributes. In your family you rather look like them, the people. His family has to be more, ahhhh, circumspect. They are rather pale and have those, ummm, rather long canines."

"Certainly is a lot of stuff to know."

"Indeed, Princess, indeed."

She laughed. "So I can wander around in public and not have to worry." She laughed even harder. "Just like I have been doing."

Ar nodded. "But, perhaps, just a little more carefully."

"O.K. Lets go get some dinner."

"This way."

In this dining room, there seemed to a number of them, Karanly and Jonathon sat waiting. They both stared as the hounds crowded in behind Dee, glanced at them, and then sat in a large cluster behind Dee as she sat.

Jonathon looked calm as calm.

Karanly stared at them.

"Family beasts." Dee pointed upwards. "There is a special area up there for them."

"Oh." Karanly started to serve the food. "Thought that maybe you had learned a summoning call of some sort."

Dee stopped chewing. "Can I do things like that?"

Jonathon choked on something.

"Of course." Karanly beamed at her. "Runs in your family." Then she glared at her brother. "You didn't tell her, did you? Anything?"

"Didn't exactly have time to do that. Yet."

"Ummmmm," said Karanly squinting at him. "Ummmm!"

"Ar?" asked Dee. "Can I do things like that?"

"Of course, Princess. It just takes some practice. We have a practice room for that. Keeps accidents or errors from doing anything, ummmm, untoward."

She took some more from a dish of chicken, at least she assumed that it was chicken, and looked across the table at Jonathon. "How many families are there?"

He swallowed what he had been chewing. "I don't think that anyone really knows that. Some of the Feyra are very secretive, or shy, or just wish to be left alone. We are not much for doing a census type of thing. I suppose if you wanted to, you could search the libraries and probably, eventually, create such a list."

He glared at his sister. "And if you keep doing things with strays our family name will be so long in a couple of centuries or so, that it will take us thirty minutes just to introduce ourself."

She grumbled back at him. "Can't let luscious like that die out. If we did, then pretty soon there wouldn't be anyone left. And that would really be boring."

Jonathon shifted his attention to Dee. "We need to visit many places yet. There is so much more we need to know. Can't have this family dying out just because that one feels like doing not nice."

It was Dee's turn to choke on something. "What? Dying out? What, not nice?"

"Seems like it," replied Jonathon. "To me."

"Oh boy," sighed Karanly. "One of those happenings."

"Huh?" said Dee.

Jonathon frowned at his sister again.

"Carnage and destruction," stated Karanly. "That family probably won't want to change their ways."

"Just when I was beginning to enjoy things," grumbled Dee.

Chapter Eight

Onward. Ever Onward.

Into The Woods. Or Something Like That.

"So, who lives in there?" Dee looked at it, so to speak. It was a hole. In a cliff. High on a mountain side.

The cliff stretched dark grey and light grey bands far to either side. There was only the one hole. Here and there, crooked and warped vegetation clung to small crevices making small green spots in all those grey tones.

"Someone who can tell us where that Messenger thing came from."

"That thing in my bedroom with two horrid voices?"

"Yes." He started for the entrance. "Do stay close."

"As glue."

"What?"

"Never mind." She glared at nothing in particular. And mumbled to herself, "A foot in two worlds and I don't understand either one now."

Deep inside the tunnel they walked. The walls

glowed dull green light. They turned a bend and stopped. At the door in the wall.

"Ummmm." Jonathon knocked politely.

"Kakmir!" growled something, somewhere.

"Well, he is home."

"What is he?" whispered Dee.

"Ummmm."

"No secrets!" she snapped.

"He is like, in a way, one of your car rental agencies. Oh! Pardon me. One of their car rental agencies."

"He rents?"

"Messengers and other, ummmm, things."

"Oh."

Jonathon thumped on the door. "Open! We have questions."

"Do dak gar pit zik!"

"SILENCE!" roared someone as the door creaked inward. A short, rather globular figure stood there, peering out, all of four feet tall, wearing a bright yellow something or other, appearing mostly like a tent turned into a garment.

"Ah hum. Do come in." The speaker backed up, and turned, speaking to them as he wobbled down the tunnel. "Don't mind the door thing. Still in training."

"Strange, strange, strange, strange," mumbled Dee to herself as she followed him, or it, or whatever, and Jonathon.

Their host dropped into a chair set next to a table

and waggled an appendage at the other chairs. As soon as they sat, a mug was shoved at each of them.

"Hondo," said Jonathon. "This is Dee." He picked up his mug and took the tiniest of sips.

Dee watched and did the same thing.

Hondo took a great swallow. "GOOD! DRINK!"

Dee keep swallowing, trying to keep her stomach under control, trying to keep it from sending its contents up and over the table and Hondo. That stuff was awful, gut wrenching horrible.

"Hondo," explained Jonathon. "Is one of the several that rents things."

"We try harder!" Hondo banged his mug on the table. Dee swallowed again. He refilled his mug and eyed theirs.

Jonathon leaned forward and spoke softly, telling Hondo what they wished to learn.

Dee listened carefully and thought that it hadn't been that long ago.

"SECRET!" bellowed Hondo. "Big, dark secret."

Jonathon leaned closer and whispered.

"A deal!" Hondo settled somewhat lower in his chair. "But no tell, ever."

"Absolutely," agreed Dee, wondering what they were agreeing to. She swallowed hard.

"Yes," said Jonathon.

Hondo wrote something on a thick piece of parchment, rolled it tight, and handed it to Jonathon. "Never no speak."

"Of course," said Dee.

"Yes," said Jonathon, standing and bowing to Hondo.

Dee lurched to her feet, swallowed hard, and bowed. "Outside,"she murmured. "Hurry."

As they stepped into the nearby meadow, she spun away and decorated a handy shrub with Hondo's drink and everything else. "Horrible. Ghastly."

Jonathon spit. Somehow he had been holding the concoction in one cheek.

She growled at him. "You could have said something."

"Ummmm, it is hard to remember that which is well known is not . . . well known."

Dee spun around and around. "Can anyone see us?"

"No."

One of the hounds appeared and ran happy wide circles around them, leaping and jumping for the joy of being outside somewhere else.

Dee laughed and slowly turned as the great beast galloped around and then up to them. "Ar told me how to do that."

Throwing her arms wide, she spun around and around, laughing and laughing. Finally she stopped, swaying from side to side, and smiled at him. "I am really beginning to like who I am. Before I was always, ummm, feeling, ah, unfinished, in a manner of speaking."

"Welcome home."

She beckoned and the gigantic beast trotted over to them, stopped, bent his head and licked her forehead.

"This is Moe," she laughed.

"Moe?"

"Ar said that he didn't know their names, or if they had any, so I named them. Manny, Moe, and Jack. And Peter." She giggled. "Peter is my editor." Moe disappeared.

"Sent him home."

He looked at her and thought that she was getting more interesting all the time.

"I have a great idea for a new D. Grant novel."

"You died."

"Huh?"

"House blew up."

"Oh. That." She shrugged. "I was on a retreat in, um, Tibet, contemplating the universe and things like that. Very mysterious, very out of touch, way deep in the Himalayas somewhere. If you are not too bad a writer but mysterious, you will do well. Critics always believe mysterious makes you better."

She looked at their surroundings. "So, what did you learn?"

"Ummmm. Hondo said my block would keep the rent-a-things away regardless of the vender. Now."

She frowned. "I suppose that is good news. Can't this guy merely send something else?"

"If he had to use rent-a-things which he seemed

to be calling up, then that is always a possibility. Of course, he could be doing all this for someone else that we haven't figured out yet."

"Aaaargh!"

"What?"

"Generic unhappy sound."

"Interesting combination."

"What is?"

"All those people, eh ah, behaviors, and you now are growing into your Feyra true person as well, ummm, slowly."

She shrugged. "Oh, ah. It is just me, pumpkin." And laughed, a very happy laugh. "I really do feel good, you know, very, very good. In spite of everything so far." She thought that was, in and of itself, quite interesting.

"We have to travel."

"Can I learn how to do that?"

He shook his head. "Your family abilities are quite different than mine."

"Damn." She hugged him. "Let's go."

"We are standing in someone's flower bed."

"Yesssssss. Can't be seen here from any window on the street. We are in a town."

"We are crushing the flowers."

"Ooop."

He led her out into the street and pointed the way.

"Where are we?"

"Small town in Bavaria. You can tell by the architecture."

"Let's find a bakery and buy some pastries then. And coffee. First."

"Ummm, we can do that."

So they did.

And sat at an inside table.

"So," she asked, "who lives here?"

"Pardosh. He specializes in house wards. He might be able to tell what that person uses and how to break through."

"Ah?"

"Yes?"

"What good are house wards if someone can do that, blab so someone can break in?"

"Ummm. Depends on the wards, who built it, or them, how it is constructed, and what they used to activate it. Your family is very adept at that. I do not believe anything, or anyone, could enter your house, no matter what they tried." He smiled at her, a soft, gentle smile, and sipped from his coffee. "You are quite safe. At home." He took another sip. "Out here, running about, is another matter."

"Would he do things like that in public?"

He nodded. "I think that one is twisted enough to behave like that."

She ate the last of her pastry. "I have been thinking."

"Yes."

"The last name in your lineage is Darthar."

"Yes. That is the original family before the change."

She nodded. "From all we found in the libraries that is my name also. I am Daliera d'Darthar Na, so far." She frowned at him. "So what are we, you and I?"

"Thousands of years ago something. Cousins of some sort or another."

He shook his head. "We haven't found the time when the split occurred where the family divided for some reason." He finished his coffee. "Ready?"

"Sure." She stood. "Let's go."

On the sidewalk, he pointed. "That one with the dark brown roof. Pardosh lives there." They strolled that way.

The door swung in as they approached.

"Do come in," said Pardosh.

He looks so ordinary, thought Dee.

They followed Pardosh into a room with a table and three chairs. Pardosh poured coffee.

Dee took a very, very careful sip. It was coffee, very good coffee, very good dark coffee.

Jonathon explained why they wished to do what they wished to do. Pardosh stared at her. Somewhere, something grumbled.

"You?"

Dee nodded.

"You are the family Darthar after the split?"

Dee nodded.

"My." He beamed at her. "My pleasure, Princess, my pleasure. All did wonder if there were any left. It has been a number of years of silence and not knowing. My, my, my, my."

Jonathon cleared his throat.

"Of course," said Pardosh, taking a scroll from somewhere and beginning to write. After a few paragraphs, he looked up. "Never to be spoken out loud. Never!" And began to write again.

When he finished, he rolled the scroll into a tight cylinder and handed it to Jonathon. "It will pop that ward wide open." He frowned at the table. "That will be the least of your problems with that problem, the very least. That family is dark, very dark, very twisted, very not nice." He shook his head slowly. "Very not nice." And smiled a wan smile at her. "Most careful, Princess, most careful."

"Many thanks." Jonathon stood.

"Yes," said Dee, standing. "Many thanks."

Outside as they strolled down the sidewalk, she looked at him. "How did he know?"

"What?"

"Princess?"

"Oh. He is a many removed cousin of your's." He whispered so none but Dee could hear, "Of the House Angorson."

"My cousin?"

"Many removed."

"Do I have many?"

Jonathon shrugged. "Once he recognized you then I knew."

"Why didn't he use my name?"

"Terribly bad manners to do that, vulgar even. Unless you introduce yourself that way. Some have died being that uncouth."

Dee sighed. "Let's go home. I am tired." Her brain felt like it should ache as she tried to remember all the information she was always being told about the Feyra and herself.

He wrapped her in his arms.

Ar opened the door as they approached and smiled at her.

She stepped in, turned, and grinned. "Do come in, Jonathon."

As he did, something dark shadow burst from the distant forest and charged at them. And splashed bits and pieces of itself all over the meadow. It had touched the house and had banged into the house wards.

"Him?" asked Dee.

"Yes," said Jonathon. "Not him but a sent thing."

"I am really starting to get irritated," grumbled Dee.

Jonathon stepped back.

"Careful," cautioned Ar.

"What? Now?" She scratched a hound behind an ear as the four of them clattered sharp talons on the floor up to them.

"I think that I will take a nap." She headed down the hall to a nearby bedroom followed by the four large beasts.

"Ummm?"

"Slowly learning," said Ar.

"Yes."

The two of them walked off to get a cup of coffee.

Feeling much better after her nap, she was once again exploring another part of the building, Ar at her side, explaining as they walked along.

"So, Ar, what else can I do?"

"What is your wish, Princess?"

"I mean things like calling the hounds."

"Ah, well, umm, you seem to have mastered call very well, very well. So, um, you can call whatever you wish, I suspect."

"You don't know?"

"One's skills vary widely, umm, depending on the particular individuals, ah, innate abilities. No."

Dee smiled at him.

Karanly laughed. "Well and cleverly done." She grinned. "Don't tell Jonathon. Surprise him, he deserves it."

Dee smiled at her. "All right." And laughed. And turned to Ar. "O.K., Ar, what is next on the tricks list?"

He gasped and drew himself up to his full height. "That, those, are not tricks! Tricks are what those people do." He waggled an arm vaguely toward the outside, frowning darkly at her. "This family does not do tricks."

"Oh. Sorry, Ar. Poor word choice."

Karanly winked at her and popped out.

Ar turned a corner and opened a door. "In here. A practice room."

Dee nodded and followed.

Inside, she twisted back and forth and looked up at the high ceiling. Then Ar started teaching.

And some time later, after much explanation and trying and failing, it was done.

"This great, Ar. Really, really great."

Then she did it, over and over and over and over again.

"I believe, Princess," said Ar. "That you have it, you really have it."

Laughing happily, she ran out into the hall and toward the far end. She giggled and looked back at Ar, running after her. "Great. Just great!"

"LOOK," he shouted as she thumped into the end of the hall and thudded in a heap to the floor. "Out."

"OOOOF!" She stood, leaned against the wall, and nodded. "Right! Always watch were you are going."

"Just so," said Ar.

"Let's have some doughnuts and coffee. To celebrate."

"This way, Princess."

They were finishing the last of the doughnuts, helped somewhat by the hound Manny who had been called to join them, when Jonathon walked in.

"Want some?" she asked.

"Ummm, maybe later. I made an appointment with Frandel. I think that he will join with us."

"A cousin?"

"Ummmmm, no. An acquaintance."

"Sure." She jumped up and thumped against him, wrapping her arms around his chest. "Let's go!"

"Ooooof ah."

"Nice place." Dee stepped away, smiling happily. "That house looks like the wicked witch's place where Hansel and Gretel had problems." She touched it. "Wonder if it is edible?"

"Frandel has a touch of whimsy." He knocked.

"Do come in, Jonathon and Dee," called someone from inside.

They walked in and were met by their host, who was wearing a tall pointed hat with an enormous feather pinned to one side. He poured three cups of coffee. "So," he said, "a big problem."

"Yes."

Frandel sipped and leaned back. "I agree. That family, if it is who I think, should be no more. He no longer follows any of our values and customs. At the rate that he is going he will call the people's attention to us and we will have to fade for a number of their generations. It was quite dull the last time. And a number of houses were ended."

He looked at Dee. "Might be why your parents lived that way, like people. I think that they felt a possibility coming and thought it best to save the family doing what they did."

He refilled their cups. And after some few quiet moments, nodded at Jonathon. "Just send a thing and tell me what I should bring. It is going to be bad. Have you asked Aranda or Big Hofga? They would enjoy the chaos. They have never liked that family for some long time ago. I am sure that they will help. They are both second sons so there is no danger to their families."

Jonathon stood. "Many thanks. We will visit them."

Dee stood. "Yes. Many thanks."

Frandel laughed. "If we survive, I might ask for a favor."

Before she could agree, Jonathon pulled her from the room and out the door. And hissed at her, "Never agree too fast, Dee. One always wishes to know with some detailed discussion as to what a favor may entail."

"Ummmm," she said.

"You are a beautiful young woman."

"Oh!"

"Yes."

She looked around. The meadow was empty.

"Wanna see something really neat?"

"Ummmm. Yes." He stepped back and away, unsure as to what this neat might be.

"Ta dah!" She hovered high above than his head, great wings beating slow. "I look like an angel with these things." She flew in a great casual circle around him and dropped lightly to the grass and kissed his cheek. The immense, white, father covered wings were gone. "Neat. Huh?"

"Ah, I suppose."

"Yep!" She stepped back. "I think that those things are where all the angel stories came from, people seeing someone like that."

He shrugged. "Well, the families weren't so careful a little time back. They didn't really start to be extremely careful until about fifty, I think."

"Fifty?"

"Ummmm, 50 A.D. in the people way of counting."

She grinned. "I wonder what is next on the Princess ability list? Ar won't say."

"Go slow, Dee, go slow. You have much time."

She frowned at him. "I suppose. But I should have been learning all this stuff when I was growing up. Right?"

He nodded. "Ummm. I think that your parents

were very clever to do what they did."

"Oh?"

"Yes. You are still alive and have the family house and Ar to teach you."

"And a real nogoodnik after me," she grumbled.

"What?"

"A not nice person."

"Ummmm. Yes." He nodded. "And so far everything that one has tried has failed. I think that one is losing control. It is good. A male out of control like that does not pay attention. Not paying attention makes one easy to kill."

Dee stared at him and winced. For a moment his eyes had glowed red.

Chapter Nine

Gathering. Preparing.

One More Place.

They stood on a high ridge, all bare rock and cold wind. Just ahead, perched on the end of that ridge, they could see a tall grey stone cylinder forty feet in diameter whose top disappeared in the low cloud cover.

"Aranda lives here."

Jonathon hurried to the door and slammed the door knocker against the wood. The thump could be heard echoing from inside.

Someone called to them. "Do come in, Jonathon and Dee."

Inside, lamps snapped into spurting flame lighting their way up the stair which spiraled up and up, following the curve of the outside wall.

Finally they came to a very low ceiling with a hatch in it. Stepping on the ladder, Jonathon threw the hatch up and over, and climbed into the next room. Dee followed.

"Wow!"

They stood in a large circular room with four

large apertures equally spaced around the high wall. The wind puffed in one opening.

"Aranda," said Jonathon.

The tall man, standing next to an even taller bird of some unusual type, smiled, long canines glistening in the light of more fluttering torches.

"A strange statement," said Aranda, looking at Dee.

"Surprise," she said. She stepped over and gently stroked the feathers on one wing. "She is beautiful. There is a pair just like this in the den for house beasts."

Aranda stared at her. "You have a pair? Den? House Beasts?" He looked past her at Jonathon. "Who is this?"

Jonathon looked past her at Aranda. "The surviving Princess of House Darthar Na."

Aranda backed up. "True speak?"

Dee smiled. Two gigantic birds coasted through one of the openings, landed, and made high pitched cooing noises at the bird already there.

"Hack and Jack," laughed Dee.

Aranda sat on the floor. "Ha nanda dah!"

"Huh?" Dee stared at him. "You look kinna pale. You sick or something?"

He wobbled to his feet. "The giant Tarken are rare. Highly treasured. This pair are your . . . house beasts?"

Dee looked at Jonathon who gave her a quick nod.

"Yes," she said. "Aren't they pretty?" She stroked one of them on the side of the neck. "Ah, maybe they ought to leave."

The pair rubbed against the other bird making soft sounds, then launched themselves out one of the openings.

"I think that they would like to visit," said Dee.

Aranda leaned against the wall and slowly shook his head.

"Oh, I am sure that they would. Don't you want them to?" She looked at Jonathon. "What did I do wrong this time?"

"Nothing."

"Visit?" mumbled Aranda. "Of course, any time you wish, any time?" He looked round-eyed at Jonathon. "You sure that you require assistance?"

"Most true, most true."

Aranda straightened up. "Then, of course. All that I can do, I will. Greatly honored." He walked over and tugged Jonathon to one side and asked, soft as soft, in his ear. "Do you think that she would?"

Jonathon shook his head. "I do not think that I would ask that at this moment."

"Ummm ah."

"Indeed. Yes."

"He seemed nice," she said as they stood at the base of the tower.

"Oh, he is." He wrapped her in his arms.

"What did you do to Aranda? His message sounded strange unsettled." Hofga glared dark fog at them.

"Just talked," said Dee, wondering what the problem was with these guys. "He didn't even offer us coffee or anything."

Hofga goggled at her. "In here! Sit! Drink!" He shoved filled cups at them as they sat.

"Thank you kindly," said Dee. She sipped. "Quite good."

Jonathon nodded.

Hofga looked at him. "Ummm?"

Jonathon explained carefully.

Hofga nodded. "That one needs killing all right. Too many houses getting unsettled. Much wondering."

Dee leaned forward. "What is really wrong with, ah . . . that one?"

"Word says a long ago promise. Other word says that one pushs that long ago promise to a wrong result. Other word says that these are wrong words. All happened long ago time, 1220 B.C. in the people marked time."

"To that one?" gasped Dee.

"Some cousin relative or other," explained Hofga. "Word says that one thinks he is that cousin relative or other."

"Ummmm," said Jonathon.

"Quite so," agreed Hofga. "How may I aid?"

Dee looked at Jonathon who said, "Wait."

Hofga nodded. "I will speak deep and wait."

"Many thanks." Jonathon stood.

Dee hastily followed suit. "Many thanks." She followed Jonathon out the door.

Two giant birds stood in the meadow, pulling shreds from something black and eating them.

"Let's go home," said Dee, grabbing him.

The birds followed in their own manner.

Dee ran inside, invited Jonathon in, and spun to face Ar. "Are all the house beasts all right?"

"Yes. All are well and healthy. Although the Furleen just arrived. Must have been a long way out."

"The Furleen?"

"Indeed. Quite rare. Your family did like to collect the rare."

Dee nodded. A large cougar-looking feline stood near them. The creature was larger than a lion with bronze colored fur and white tiger stripes on its neck and shoulders.

"Wow, that is some pussy cat!"

It flowed over and bumped her with its head, almost tumbling her from her feet.

"Hey! Careful there!"

It sat and looked at her, great, staring green eyes.

She rubbed its neck. "Really soft and plush fur."

It rumbled happy at her.

"Ar, how do all these beasts manage to stay out of sight?"

"They are very good at that, Princess. Much better than some members of some houses have been not too far long ago." He frowned. "That caused problems did those ones. Started all kinds of nonsense believing among the people. Some of that hasn't died out yet." He sighed.

Dee nodded. The Furleen was gone. "That the last of the beasts?"

"Most true, Princess, most true."

"Let's eat dinner." She tugged Jonathon down the hall.

Dee woke well rested and felt a warm body lying in bed with her. "Jonathon?" She jerked upright. It better not be!

The Furleen looked at her and blinked. The great beast was flat on its side, stretched out in luxurious repose.

Well, thought Dee, it is certainly a large bed, but not that big. "Off, off, off."

It flowed liquid smooth off and sat and looked at her.

She jerked the covers up to her neck. And sent her back to the beast quarters. She didn't go.

Dee waggled one hand. "Shoo!"

She didn't shoo.

"Go away."

"No."

"What?" She goggled at her.

"No."

"You can speak?"

"Shhhhh," rasped the Furleen. "Family secret. Not even Ar knows that."

"Oh, me," sighed Dee. "Another one. So, why won't you go away?"

"Not nice things lurk outside the house. It is a house beast's duty to guard family members."

"You didn't guard my parents."

"Different. They moved themselves outside the pale, so to speak."

"O.K. What is outside the house?"

"Not nice things. Sent by that one, the not nice one you ought to kill." The beast seemed to smile as it licked its lips. "Be glad to help, Princess." She looked at the door. "Ar comes." And faded into the wallpaper.

"Now that is truly amazing," mumbled Dee as the door popped open.

"Princess," gasped Ar. "The house is under siege by not nice things."

"Oh. Anything that I can do?"

"Come eat breakfast," urged Ar. "No."

"Be right there. After I get dressed."

Ar looked uncomfortable and left the room.

"Ever stranger," grumbled Dee, hurrying into her clothes. "Every time that I get used to it, it just gets stranger and stranger." Great green eyes watched her from the wallpaper.

Over breakfast, she looked out the large window

as strange things, very ugly strange things, prowled back and forth in the large meadow.

She looked at Jonathon. "Same guy?"

"Yes." He munched on another piece of toast.

"Do you have any idea what this ding bat thinks that he is doing?"

Jonathon stared at her. Such a strange dialect she had.

"Ah," she said, "that not nice one."

"Oh." He looked at her and decided her speech patterns must have come from having lived among the people for some time.

"Yes, him," he said.

"Do you think that we could convince that one to stop doing stuff like that!" She pointed at the meadow and the prowling things.

"No."

"Can't we get rid of those . . . whatever they are, out there." She waved her toast at the window.

"Ah ummmmmm."

"Humpf," replied Dee.

Ar looked shocked.

"Now what?" she grumbled, wondering which of the cultural taboos she had stepped on this time. "Don't the Feyra have the equivalent of Emily Post somewhere?"

Two blank expressions and a pair of green eyes stared at her.

"Ah, never mind," she mumbled. "Maybe it

would be a good project when I have time."

"The things can't do anything," stated Jonathon.

"Ummmmm?" said Dee.

"Yes?"

"Couldn't we do the same thing back? Take that one's mind off us for awhile?"

"My goodness," gasped Ar.

"Ummmmm," said Jonathon. "I will ask Hofga."

By the time that they had finished relaxing over their coffee, the meadow was empty.

"Most clever, Princess," said Ar.

"Turn about is fair play," stated Dee, watching the great thing flow from the mural on the wall and sit near her. "Cheshire Cat," she said to her.

She winked.

"What's next?"

"Research."

She stood. "Let's go."

"So, where are we this time?"

The structure, all moss covered pale stone, bay windows and towers, stood at the edge of a cliff looking down at the ocean.

"Ummmm, Sweden, I think that they call it."

They walked inside and were greeted by a short and rather wide woman dressed in bright red clothes. "Welcome, how may I aid you in your research?"

Jonathon leaned close and whispered.

"Oh, that one."

He nodded.

"Family atlas files are up this way, all the maps are up a few." She nodded as she started up the broad staircase. "I am sure that we can find just what you need. Word says that someone has hungry eyes on some poor female. Perhaps you might be able to dissuade that one to stop making trouble like that."

Dee jerked.

"We will try," stated Jonathon.

The pair were dust and grime coated up to their elbows from shuffling maps and other sheets from pile to pile to pile before Jonathon smiled. He tapped a map. "Nice spot. Hidden in plan sight." He made a few notes and stood.

Dee looked up and out a window. The stars were shining in the night sky. "Time certainly flies by." Her stomach grumbled. "Boy, am I ever hungry." She stretched and stretched. "Let's go."

"Outside," said Jonathon.

They stepped outside.

Something grabbed her.

Chapter Ten.

Some Surprise This Is.

Dark and Dingy A Place.

"Get your hands off, ugly butt!" snarled Dee as she kicked it on the side of one misshapen foot and slapped its hand.

Surprised, it did.

"Where are we?" she demanded.

"Captive," it grunted.

"And dumb besides ugly," she grumbled.

She looked around. Not much to see. Dark stone everything. Only one door made of grey wood. It stood in front of the door.

She waved a hand at it. "Stand aside, lump!"

"You captive! You no go!"

"Boy," she mumbled, "do I ever need to know some offensive skills." She looked up at it and glared. "You going to get out of the way?"

"No go!"

Moe looked over her shoulder at it and snarled.

The thing screeched, spun, and ran for safety. Taking the door, the door jamb, and goodly portion of the attaching wall with it as it hurtled away, down the corridor outside.

Dee carefully stepped through the ruble and onto the clean floor and peered into the distance. "Thanks, Moe. Guess that there is only one way to go." As they walked into the dim, she sighed. "Now all I need are a Scarecrow, a Tin Woodman, and a Cowardly Lion."

Moe wagged his tail.

They passed through two more shattered doors and three bends in what Dee decided was some kind of a tunnel. Far in the distance they heard a crashing sound.

"I think that whoever is responsible for this place," she said to Moe, "likes to play Dungeons and Dragons."

Jonathon stood and stared into the night, his anger building and building. He was very, very unhappy. Overhead, dark clouds were gathering, lightning dancing from cloud to cloud. All around him, in all directions, anything that could flee, did.

Karanly gently tapped him on one shoulder. "Brother, calm down. Now, please."

His head snapped around, his eyes glared red fire at her. But he did. Calm down. Great wings folded, claws retreated, he dwindled into himself. Then he was just Jonathon again.

She looked up as the clouds drifted away and faded. "Much better." Stepping around, she smiled at him. "We ought to be able to follow her path. I don't think that the agent was that clever or cautious."

He kissed her on the forehead and took her hand.

Dee peered carefully around the next turn in the tunnel. Bright light flooded from an open door beyond which she could see a rather pleasant appearing room.

She patted Moe on the side. "Do you know how to hide?"

The great hound sat.

Dee nodded. "Hum."

The Furleen sat next to him.

"I thought that something sneaky was required."

"Of course," said the gigantic feline, standing, walking over, and fading into the rock pattern and silently oozing around the door jamb and into the room.

Dee followed and squinted at the man standing there, dressed entirely in black.

"Who are you, short, dark, and handsome?"

He was all of that as he leaned one shoulder ever so casually against the wall. He smiled, gleaming white teeth, eyes scanning up and down.

"I am Arza ta'Qarna Farthan, Princess." He nodded.

"You the guy causing all the trouble, blowing up my house, things like that there?"

"Humble apologies for that antak dwelling. But, no one may affect your true house."

"Ummmmmmm. Then, you can just knock off all

the bother! It is really irritating having your ugly things around all the time. Go bother someone else!"

"Princess d'Darthar Na, we are cross-tie from some time past."

"If true, it was really a bad idea. Some time past? When?"

"About the time the people were finally figuring out how to write, ah, in their peculiar time marking system about 6000 B.C., plus or minus a thousand." He waggled one hand casually. "More or less."

"Well, cutie pie, I really do not like you, regardless of how long ago whatever it was that happened. Your behavior is atrocious. Just demanding this or that is a real turn off." She spun slowly around. "So, where is the door out of here? How do I get out of this place? That tunnel was an awfully dumb idea."

He stared at her. She spoke a strange dialect. Some of her words had no meaning. Why would she call him after some sort of dessert pie? This was not going as he thought that it should. She was certainly as beautiful as the females of that family always were. Her offspring would be handsome, a welcome and needed addition to his house. But she didn't seem to understand his need or her debt as he saw it. After all, the way he saw things were all that mattered. He was The Head of a new house after all.

"DOOR!" she snapped, breaking into his thoughts. "OUT! Where is the door out? Hello there! Stop day dreaming and pay attention!"

He straightened up. And glowered green glow at her.

"That makes you look ill." She giggled. "Sorta sea sick looking."

Karanly and Jonathon looked around.

"Doesn't look like much of a wine cellar," observed Karanly. "Wonder what smashed that door?"

They walked over the rubble and started down the long tunnel.

"You know," suggested Dee, as she finished thumping all the walls searching for a hidden door she assumed had to be there, somewhere. "If you weren't such an egomaniac I could have invited you over for lunch, or dinner, and we could have discussed things in a civilized manner."

She stepped up and rapped a knuckle on his sternum. "Having things popping into my bedroom, waking me up, and ripping my clothes off is not a very flattering way to meet someone." She gave him another thump. "So, what's your problem? You spoiled? An only child?"

He jerked back and into the wall. Two green eyes peered at him just over the top of his head. This female was not what he had expected. She didn't seem to know her place. She was bad mannered. Her parent's had certainly not raised her very well. Maybe they should have lived longer. Perhaps that had been a mistake.

And she apparently had become attached to that ugly dwelling, that ugly people dwelling. Most peculiar for one of the Feyra.

"Princess! Stop! You must stop this instance! I am tired of your speaking so!" He glared at her.

"Tough it out, smart guy."

He beckoned in a Harkar "You are coming with me, Princess. Willingly or not."

She stepped back, away from the thing's claws as it reached for her. "Moe, come in and growl at this thing, will you?"

"Moe?" He frowned at her, and gasped, "At ka!"

The hound had stepped in and peered over the top of her head. The Harkar disappeared.

"How did that get in here?"

Dee smiled. "I found him."

"Why weren't you eaten? What is going on in here?"

"He likes me. Time for me to go. Where's the way out?"

He glowered at her. "Do you not understand? This place is mine. You are mine. And I will do whatever I wish to do with mine! Can you understand that? Female!" He crossed his arms over his chest and looked lordly at her.

"Pa bak!" she snapped.

"A useless curse," he snarled, changing, and reached long talons for her. "AK!"

Two great fur covered paws clenched his

shoulders and the edge of his neck.

A great cat head snapped his head off. Except he was no longer there.

"Great," grumbled Dee. "Now how do I get out of here?"

Karanly stepped through the door and scratched Moe behind an ear and grinned at Dee. "We can do that. Who were you talking to?"

"A very obnoxious stuck up guy who called himself Arza ta'Qarna Farthan."

Karanly looked around the room.

"He left. Suddenly," said Dee.

"Pa bak!" snarled Jonathon. "Why didn't you kill him?"

"Forgot to carry a gun. Let's go home. Please?"

House Darthar Na.

Sitting at a table for a late dinner, they talked.

"He told you his true name?" asked Jonathon.

"If that is what it was," replied Dee, starting on her dessert.

"Wonder why he would do something like that?" Karanly licked the frosting from her lips.

"He said that I was coming with him, willing or not."

"Why didn't he take you away?" asked Jonathon.

"Moe stared at him and Purr Cat grabbed him and tried to snap off his head. But he wasn't there."

Jonathon sighed. "He is much too confident. He

must have someone helping him."

"He is an egomaniac," grumbled Dee. "And crazy sounding."

"Even so. Must have help. Of some kind. We need to find out. And be very cautious. Very, very cautious." He looked at her. "You were lucky because he was over confident. I doubt that he will be again."

"He thinks we have some sort of agreement dating from around 6000 B.C. or thereabouts. He can't be that old."

Karanly laughed. "No, he is more recent. 1420 A.D., I think, as the people figure time."

Dee's mouth dropped open. "Don't you guys age or die?"

Jonathon smiled. "He will. Die."

Dee stood and beckoned Karanly. "We need to talk. Just you and I." She headed out and down the hall and into one of the other rooms.

As soon as they sat, Dee said, "O.K. first question. What did you do with Kraz?"

"Not much. If he died without offspring then it would have been the end of his family. So I just helped him out. There are too few families as it is."

"Uh huh. How does one help him out in just a few days?"

Karanly flapped a hand over her mouth and stared at Dee. The hand slowly dropped. "Didn't your mother tell you anything?"

"About what?"

"You know. Having children and things?"

"Of course. But that doesn't explain a few days."

"It was the usual four days." Karanly frowned at her. "No offense, Princess, but I think your mother did a poor job."

"The usual four days? Ummmmmm, why don't you just tell me, ah, what ever, about the usual four days?"

"Of course." Karanly smiled. "Really not much to tell. First, the male fertilizes the female. You know about that?"

"Of course!"

"Then in two days, you lay your egg, and . . . "

"WAIT!"

"What?"

"Egg. Explain egg, please."

"Well, it takes two days. The first day can be uncomfortable. The second day can get painful, very painful, depending upon how large the egg gets. They grow so rapidly. Then, you lay it, keep it warm for two days, it hatches, and in this case, he raises the child." She beamed. "See. Simple. Takes no time at all. Just four days."

Dee slumped. "No. I do not see. How can you lay eggs?"

Karanly laughed. "Oh, that. Boy, did your mother not do her duty. You know what a platypuss is? Warm blood and lays eggs?"

Dee nodded. "Sure. So?"

"We are like that, some. The people went in another direction, developed all that complicated and messy process, dragging around a growing new child for nine months. But there is one thing that you have to pay attention to though. The rapidly growing egg pushes stuff around so you don't feel hungry. But you use up vast quantities of energy because the process is so fast. So the families always see to it that there is always a great meal available and ready. Once the egg is laid you will be ravenous. You should immediately eat until you don't feel hungry or your hunger can overwhelm you. In the very long ago, before the rooms, some females became so crazed that they even ran off and attacked people. And in the not so long ago as well as some of the houses were not too careful. That is what started all those nonsense stories about werewolves and vampires and such attacking at night. So just have a large meal handy and it won't be a problem."

"So, just eat a lot?" said Dee, nodding.

"Karthan," said Karanly. "I think that I had better tell you about that as well."

"O.K. Now what?" She sighed. It seemed like there was always one more thing.

"It is a female thing."

"Oh. Another female thing? Like eating a lot? Having rapidly growing eggs in your gut?"

Karanly nodded. "It is a female thing that happens whenever we are reproducing. But it only lasts until the egg hatches and we have replenished our energy level. But it is something that you must know about."

Dee sighed, and wondered, now what? The idea of laying eggs was strange enough.

"Way long ago," began Karanly. "Way long ago back during our very primitive days, this sort of thing was something the females did. We, the females, were the predators, a rather large predator when we had to hunt, and brought home the meat. Now it has, ah, degenerated, so to speak, to just those few days when we are having children."

Dee nodded, still wondering.

"I told you about the danger of the hunger. That is part of Karthan. Back in those ever so long ago days, when the first houses were finally being built, they were always built with a special set of rooms which we still have in every house. These rooms had, and have, heavy, very thick, outside wooden doors, doors that open on the hall outside. These doors have great latches only on the outside. The interior connecting door between the two rooms can only be unlatched from that hallway. The female just fertilized goes into those rooms and is locked in. Two days later, the door between the rooms was unlatched from the outside hall allowing access to the table next door piled high with food. It was filled during the first two days when the latch was in place. The mother can then feed and take care of that terrible hunger, as well as the first feeding of the offspring after the hatching, which happens two days after the egg is laid. Then the outer door is unlatched and mother and offspring reenter the house. Four days all together. And no more hunger crazed females frightening everything."

"Why go through all that?"

"Karthan is a physiological change that the species still undergoes. For a long time, until we trained the daughters better, it was too frightening for the mothers to know about themselves that way."

"What?" Dee banged one fist on the table top. "Now what? What way?"

"It is just our original great predator form." Karanly laughed. "Let's put it this way. Nothing ever wants to disturb or anger a Karthan."

Dee sighed as tears ran down her cheek as she looked at Karanly. "This is getting to be too much. Are there many more things like that, like turning into some sort of terrifying predator mother, that I don't know about? Yet?"

Karanly shrugged. "Every house has things no one else knows, in detail. So I can't say." She reached across the table and patted one of Dee's hands. "I know you are finding all this to be overwhelming when you thought that you were just one of the people, and that all this is quite a shock. But I keep trying to think of things, sorta basic, that you should know." She refilled their cups, leaned back, and took a sip. "Ever since coffee was discovered by the people we have drunk a lot of it. Something in it has a great appeal to us."

Dee slumped deeper and mumbled, "So I lay eggs?"

"Of course." Karanly nodded. "If that one, that not nice one ever manages to fertilize you, if it was me, I would just break the egg right away before you start to keep it warm. It would serve him right. Then he would have to wait for some long time before he could even try that again. Plenty of time to kill him." She grinned.

"Do I cluck?"

Karanly grinned at her. "No. Not us."

"Stranger, stranger, stranger, stranger," Dee mumbled. Then she shoved herself upright. "Now explain that one's age. Please?"

Karanly frowned.

"I don't understand his age," said Dee.

Karanly leaned forward and looked at her, deep frown. "You know what I think, Princess. I think that when your parents fled to pretend to be people that they wiped away your memory so you would like to be people. Sounds to me that they were very desperate to protect you."

Dee shook her head. "Let's just skip that for a moment. Age. Tell me about that."

"Sure. What?"

"When was I born, ummmm, hatched?"

"We say born."

"O.K., born."

Karanly looked somewhere for a bit. "I do

believe it was right around 1500 B.C. as the people figure time. That one who bothers is your junior by some. Maybe that one has a fetish for older females."

"1500 B.C.," gasped Dee. "I am only thirty-eight."

Karanly gurgled laughter. "That is why there are so very few of us. Children are widely spaced in terms of time."

"But how can anything live that long?"

Karanly shrugged.

"And I should know all this and all that and everything else?"

"Oh my yes. Of course."

"Ar!" snapped Dee.

He appeared next to her left side. "Princess?"

"Explain memory wipe to me, my memory wipe."

He tilted to one side and sagged. "Oh, dear. You know about that?"

"We sorta figured it out."

"You won't exile me, will you? That is what your parents threatened me with."

Karanly gasped and went pale. She cleared her throat and spoke to Dee. "That is like a forever lingering death."

"No, Ar. You are safe. Just explain."

So he did. How her parents had fled for her safety and felt that was the only way to hide her among the people. To insure that she believed that she was one of them, they created an entire people memory and replaced her true memories.

"Can you undo it, Ar?"

"Alas, no. Once done, forever done." He smiled at her. "But you are coming right along, for, ahem, such a short period of time."

"Think that I will go to bed." Dee stood and wondered from the room.

Karanly glared at him. "Will she be all right?"

Ar glared back. "Of course! It is my duty to see that it is so."

Dee woke and stared at the ceiling, nudged the warm body sprawling over half of the bed, and grumbled, "Don't you have a cat bed upstairs?"

"This is safer for you and nicer for me," said Purr Cat, stretching and stretching.

She nudged her with a knee, "Move over, bed hog." And grumbled at nothing in particular. "So, now I am a Sequoia. How can anyone live that long? This is all crazy, crazy stuff. Just crazy, crazy stuff."

Purr Cat rolled onto her back, legs flopping in all directions. "It is just the way things are, Princess. It is why the families worry so much about children. The families are usually small. Loss of a member is a major disaster because there is such a long time between having children. Long ago by anyone's measure of time, there were many more of you. It took your species thousands of years to realize what they were and to develop cultural rules of behavior before they all went extinct."

Dee sighed. And sat up. "Takes a lot to suddenly get used to for someone starting as a child, a very old child."

Purr Cat purred laughter and flowed liquid soft to the floor and stood by the door.

Dee washed, dressed, and headed down the hall to eat breakfast, the Furleen by her side.

As all sat sipping coffee after breakfast, Dee said, "Let's go outside. I want to try something."

"Ummmmm." Jonathon stood.

Not too far from the bottom of the stairs, they stopped.

"Is it safe out here?" Dee searched the vast meadow for unwelcome things.

"For now."

"O.K." Dee smiled. "That guy told me his true name. So I am going to see if I can call him here. Get ready, here we go."

A figure appeared. Jonathon clamped both hands around his throat.

Dee gasped. "He isn't him. Who is he?"

Jonathon eased his grip. "Who are you? True name speak!"

"I am," rasped the man, all harsh indignity. "Arza ta'Qarna Farthan." He frowned at them, then ordered, "Release me!"

"Can't be," snapped Dee. " He is shorter, dark, handsome, dresses all in black."

Arza wrenched himself from Jonathon's grasp. "That is the wretched third son of House Parthandar. He told you my true name? Who pulled me here? Who can do things like that? Unheard of!" He huffed and looked down his nose and frowned dark glare at them.

"Ummmm," said Jonathon. "Word comes that Arza is not nice and many feel needs killing."

Arza shook, face going even more pale. "That one has gone too far, for too long. The several families thought it to be merely third son behavior, youthful behavior, soon to be grown out of." He glared at them. "Who are you?" he demanded.

"Jonathon."

"Dee."

Arza nodded. "Good enough for now. We must counsel."

Jonathon nodded so Dee opened the door and invited them in.

Jonathon gently touched Arza on the shoulder as they headed down the hall to a comfortable room to sit and talk in. "If you lie or attempt harm, your family will mourn you."

"May I ask whose house I am in?"

Jonathon nodded.

Dee opened a door and waved them inside. "This is House Darthar Na." And served them coffee.

Arza dropped into a chair. "Darthar Na was a well liked house, many special skills" He nodded at her. "You did that, made the call?"

She nodded. "I knew your true name but didn't realize the misinformation."

Arza nodded again. "It may be to the good. That one has doomed himself. That behavior is the worst not nice, most!"

Jonathon held out his cup. Dee poured. He said, "Someone has to be working with him, has to be."

"Who?"

"Know not."

Arza looked at Dee. "May I leave?" She nodded. He was gone.

She looked around the table. "Do any of you understand anything about your, ummm, our species?"

He shook his head. "We have had some study long ago and often to figure it out. None have, so far. There are no early records, there have been no fossils found. Much of our genetics is like the people, some is not like anything else."

He shrugged. "Perhaps we are just some fluke of nature among all the other flukes that have appeared and disappeared, but for some reason no one yet understands, we survived instead of disappearing."

Jonathon laughed. "We are quite strange as a species. But here we are, still alive, and surviving. We survived, therefore we are, to paraphrase Descartes." His eyes searched her face. "We live. What else can we do? I, for one, prefer it over the alternative."

Dee sighed. And nodded. "Right."

She scratched Purr Cat behind an ear. She had appeared and was now standing close to Dee, head propped on the table, eyeing the bacon.

"We have to find that one's helper," said Jonathon.

"How?"

"More research."

"O.K." She stood, slid the bacon platter over, and said, "Let's go."

Chapter Eleven

Searching. Ever Searching.

Houses. Here and There.

"Sweden again?"

Jonathon nodded. "Need to research that family Parthandar. We have been going in the wrong direction for too long."

"That guy is pretty sneaky."

"Uummmmm." He knocked on the door and they were ushered in. Jonathon gave the librarian the family name and the pair were led deep into a timber clad hall, all panels and warm lighting.

In a side room, the librarian gestured. "Those with the green binding." He left.

One shelf had nothing but thick volumes with green bindings stacked on it.

Dee stepped sideways. "Tell me what we need to know and I will start at this end. You can start at the other end."

He told her and they started. And slowly they filled numbers of pages with notes.

"Lots of children in that family."

"Ummm." He lifted out another book and opened it and began to take notes.

She stuffed a volume back on the shelf and took down another thick book and dropped it on the table. "Let's get something to eat."

He looked up. "Yes."

The librarian appeared and guided them down and around and into a room with food set for two, bowed and left.

Jonathon discussed all that they had found out, so far.

"He has two brothers and two sisters, all older. So, in many ways he is the least child in terms of family matters, inheritance, and inter-family agreements."

"So?" Dee poured coffee into their cups.

"So, I think that he wishes to start a new family, one where he would be the first male and head. I think that when you two were very small you probably played that game, all the children do, let's start a new family. He seems to have never forgot you and appears to believe a child's game is an adult's reality."

"Think so?"

Jonathon nodded. "Families with small new children often have gatherings as part of the children's socialization and understanding of other families abilities, sub-cultural differences, and belief systems."

Dee chewed thoughtfully on something. "That is how it is done, huh?"

"Yes." He emptied his cup and stood. "Let's see

what else the remaining volumes can tell us. We need his true name and maybe something that will give us a hint as to who is working with him. Then we have to find the lists that will tell us which families can call and control a Capture thing. Not everyone can."

"Lists?"

"Yes. We have in the Hall of Lists, listings of abilities. It is useful if you want something, or some ability, you don't have. You can get help from those who can or will. Then maybe one of those families will ask you for help some other time. There is a lot of trading back and forth."

"So, you think this, ummm, not nice person wants to start a new family and is working with someone you might find on a list?"

"Yes."

"Is starting a new family a bad thing to do?"

"Not at all. It happens every time or so. But never this way."

He stared at her. "The families discuss who the son, or daughter, should mate with, and from which family. It is often thought to be best to find a cross-tie that will benefit the new family and the cross-tie one. He appears to be going his own way without family knowledge and involvement. And he certainly hasn't consulted with you." He frowned at the table top.

"What?"

"This behavior is going to damage his helper or helpers as well. I do not think that they understand that.

Yet!"

He smiled at her, a soft, gentle smile. "My sister is impulsive, but she knew in terms of family interests that your cousin, now Kraz a'Darthar d'Anathar, was acceptable to the family."

Dee nodded, filing away one more piece of cultural behavior to remember. It seemed to her that with their long life spans The Feyra had created some rather Byzantine cultural systems of family behavior. She decided that it was time to make a journal with a cross-reference index.

"Where to now?"

He stood. "The Hall of Lists."

She laughed. "Of course, the Hall of Lists."

He stared at her.

"Let's go," she said. And grabbed him.

"Ooof!"

They stood in a forest of gigantic trees. They appeared to be in a grove of Redwoods.

She giggled. "Members of the family."

Jonathon frowned.

"Hard to explain." Dee shrugged. "Where is it?"

He pointed. It was similar than the others but with a thicker trunk. He stepped up and rapped on it. A door opened and someone called, "Do come in."

After walking up a very long spiral staircase barely illuminated by missing knotholes in the outer skin, they stepped into a large room. On all sides were racks of scrolls.

"The Hall of Lists," said Jonathon. He stepped over and talked in low tones with the Keeper of Lists, who wandered around until he had gathered up the scrolls that had what Jonathon was looking for.

They sat at a small table as Jonathon opened one of the scrolls. Then he told her what to write down and the house name.

"Ummmm." He sat back as the last scroll snapped shut. "Only five names. Capture things must be a rare skill. But it makes our search that much easier. Only five families to visit."

"Now?"

"No. Back to your house. Food and rest. We can start tomorrow."

Over dinner they discussed the things they had found and the five houses that they now had to visit. Jonathon said that only one, Quartep, he personally knew. The other four, Adantender, Mbanar, Obiteon, and Bockten, he only knew as family names. So they would visit Quartep and then have to do research on the others, their values, and locations.

When they finished, Dee told him good-night and left, having decided to walk up a few levels and try a bedroom up there. As she wandered along the third level outside hall, she wondered why the house had so many bedrooms if most of the Feyra families were so small. The hall bent to the left and then to the right. She turned into the first, a large bedroom with large windows along the outside wall.

Dee stood and looked out at a clear night sky with a large moon flooding down soft silver.

"Ar, come here please?"

He appeared. "Princess?"

"Why does this house have so many bedrooms, and for that matter, so many rooms at all?"

"Ah ummm."

Dee sighed. "Not more strange?"

"Oh no, not at all."

"Well?" She glanced sideways at him.

"In the quite long ago your family would visit other families and often a rather large number of families would visit here. This house was known as one of having great hospitality."

"And now?"

Ar stared out the window. "Since not long ago the families have tended toward self-isolation. I do believe it is because that when your parents fled into the people that the shock of that started the closing in, so to speak."

"So we could, if we wished, invite the families to visit again?"

"Yes. With one, um ah, problem."

"Figures," she grumbled. "What is it? Now?"

"Wellll, ummm, it seems that your parents, ummmm, hid the House Book somewhere. You need it. It lists all those who are welcome to visit."

Dee leaned her forehead on the window. "Ar, do you have any idea what was causing my parents to behave the way they did?"

"No, Princess. Only this, and nothing more. Something very dark was occurring, something that they were very afraid of, afraid for your survival. I do believe you only bumped into the edge of that great dark with the third son."

Ar leaned close to her. "Please, Princess, great caution. You and Jonathon are touching that very dark. If you die, I will be doomed to live in an ever empty house. That last long time was very not nice, all hollow space and emptiness. I could have helped if only they had told me." He dragged a sleeve across his eyes. "Humble pardon, Princess."

Dee turned and threw an arm around his shoulders. "I am so sorry, Ar, so very sorry. I really am." She patted his shoulder. "May I ask a favor?"

"But of course. I am your's to command. Always."

"Then I want you to systematically search this place for that missing book whenever Jonathon and I are gone. We need to find the House Book and any other journals or what ever will help explain what was happening then. Maybe those things have the real information that we need."

Ar smiled. "A pleasure."

"Thanks, Ar. See you in the morning. Goodnight."

Ar bowed and was gone.

Dee soaked in a tub of hot water and lots of bubbles, crawled into bed, and fell asleep thinking that they were finally headed in the correct direction.

She slept undisturbed. And unaware of the shape that floated outside and peered at her through the large window.

Chapter Twelve

Lots Of Visiting To Do.

Another Large House.

"So, where are we?"

Dee looked up and down the street. It was an avenue of mansions, large, sprawling, multi-story edifices.

"This," said Jonathon, indicating one with his chin, "is House Quartep. That family spent some long time in northern Africa."

He pushed open the gate and led her around to the side door.

"Are all these places along here Feyra?"

"No. Just this house." He thumped on the door. "They will have to relocate soon before their neighbors begin to wonder about them. That is the problem when one lives among the people. Their life spans are so different."

The door swung open. "Jonathon and friend, do come in."

"This is Dee," said Jonathon.

"Dee, most welcome. I am Vierda." The tall

woman kissed Jonathon on the cheek. "It has been a little time. Coffee?"

"Yes."

She led them down the hall and into a room, waited until they took a seat, then poured and handed them their cups before she sat.

She took a sip. "So?"

"This family can call Capture things, true?"

She nodded.

"Is any here working with someone else?"

"We do not do that!" She glared at him and at the idea that they would.

Jonathon waggled his free hand. "Had to ask. We have quite a puzzle to solve. Someone with that skill is working with someone not nice."

Vierda gasped. "How do you know that?"

"Because," said Dee, "someone grabbed me with one."

"Oh, dear." Vierda refilled their cups. "We would never allow something like that. Never!" She smiled. "Especially to a friend of Jonathon's. Do I know your house?"

Dee looked at Jonathon who nodded.

"My house," said Dee, "is House Darthar Na."

Vierda's cup rattled on the table top as she set it down. "Darthar Na! All believed that house to be extinct. For some time ago."

Dee shrugged and took a sip from her cup. "Well, I guess all just thought wrong."

"Ummmm," said Jonathon. "Long story. We shall visit soon. Spend some time."

Vierda nodded. And smiled at Dee. "Do come as well. I would be ever so interested to hear how you come to be, ah, alive, after we heard such a wrong tale."

Dee nodded.

Jonathon stood. "We have to be off. Nice to see you again, Vierda." He headed for the door. "We have much to do."

Outside he grabbed Dee and took her away.

To a dark forest.

"Something most wrong, Dee."

"I'll say. Ar told me that the reason my parents fled is that there was something very dark occurring. And whatever it was must have been very not nice. He also added that he thought the edge of it all was that third son we bumped into."

"Ummmm ah."

"My place?"

She opened the door and invited him in, and led him to a comfortable room with a large outside window and filled two cups, shoving one across the table to him.

"Now what?"

"Vierda was nervous because you were still alive. Daliera, it seems that you are the focus, now, and some time ago. That third son is being used by someone, or a group of someones, the very dark that Ar mentioned."

He sipped and pushed his cup over for a refill. She poured and returned it to him.

"The families," he began, "have always been fairly independent from long ago after a, ummmm, great disagreement about organization and decision making. Some wished to have a structure with only some houses making the decisions for all, mainly the same ones wanting that structure. A number of families went extinct during that disagreement."

He slumped, just a little, and looked at her with sad sad eyes. "It appears that your parents ran out into the people and hid, an act that disrupted some sort of power grab." He gulped his coffee. "Now it seems that their daughter plays a key role, somehow, in these plans that were once disorganized by your disappearance, and assumed death."

"But now I am alive and those unknowns are back at it, whatever it is."

"Yes."

"Boy," sighed Dee, "was my life as one of the people ever so simple, once upon a time."

"That third son might know more than he is supposed to."

"What?"

Jonathon straightened up and leaned toward her. "It seems the knowledge of you being alive is not spreading through the families as fast as news of that much excitement usually does." He sighed. "This is going to be hard, very hard. So, this is what we, you and I, are going to do." And he began to explain in some detail.

As they ate breakfast the next morning, after turning in early to get as much rest as they could, Ar reported on his search.

"The entire ground floor is done. I found a few papers scattered here and there but no books. I will put everything in the main library."

Dee nodded. "Thanks, Ar."

Ar left to start on the next floor up.

Jonathon handed her a slip of paper.

She nodded, and stood, headed for the main entry, Jonathon walking by her side

Just past the base of the stairs, in the grass covered meadow, cropped short by some type of grazer over night, they stopped. The four hounds stood around them.

Dee read the slip of paper.

Aranda appeared. Then Hofga and Frandel.

Aranda smiled at his friends and at Jonathon. "Didn't know that you could do that, Jonathon."

Jonathon shook his head.

Aranda jerked and stared at her. "You?"

Dee strode up and inside, invited all to come in and told her visitors, "You are going to have large company for awhile. One of the hounds will always be with you."

Hofga glared at her. "Hak pata!"

"Could go home, I suppose," she suggested. She beckoned them down the hall into a comfortable room so they could sit and talk.

As they settled in the large, comfortable chairs, coffee cups in hand, Jonathon began.

"You three are the closest friends I have. The hounds are, umah, merely a precaution." He held up his free hand to stop the comments before they could start.

"There is a great dark building, somewhere, and I do not know who is involved or why. I fear House Quartep may be involved."

"Vierda?" gasped Frandel. "Oh, Jonathon!"

"Perhaps." Jonathon shrugged.

"Ummmmm, I see," said Aranda, glancing sideways at the hound sitting there.

"Yes." Jonathon nodded. "I would like you three to remain here while Dee and I talk with the Houses Andantender, Mbanar, Obiteon, and Brockten."

"Surely not Brockten," grumbled Hofga. "I have known Trygant for some long time. Doesn't strike me as one who would be involved in some underdark organization,"

"Five houses," stated Jonathon, "can call Capture things. One or more of them is involved in some manner or other. I intend to find out who and what!" He looked from face to face. "This is a most not nice time. I fear the end of some houses before it settles."

"Oh, ah, mung," hissed Frandel.

"Careful cautious worry," explained Jonathon. "Think deep, friends. Think deep." He stood. "Until morning next." He bowed to them and walked from the room.

Dee stood and looked from shocked face to shocked face. "Till morning next then. Ar will show you to your bedrooms. They are quite comfortable." She smiled. "Come on, Moe, let's take a walk." The pair left the room and wandered down the hall.

The three looked at each other.

Frandel cleared his throat and poured more coffee for them. "Hard to believe."

Hofga grumbled at him. "Ah ummmm, if Jonathon says something is so then I believe it! This will be messy, very, very messy. Morning then." He stomped from the room. Manny followed him.

Aranda stood after emptying his cup in one long swallow. "Hofga is correct about messy. Fran, Jonathon is getting a very unsettled look in his eyes, a very not nice thing to see." He nodded. "Going to need all the help that he can get."

Frandel wobbled to his feet. "Folk never learn from past errors. The last time it happened five houses went extinct and eight almost followed. Long lives don't seem to enhance wisdom, do they?"

Each was guided to the appropriate bedroom by Ar.

In another small room Jonathon turned to Dee, "Can you really hear what the hounds hear?"

She nodded. "That is a closely guarded family secret never before shared. Ar wasn't very comfortable that you would know about that, very uncomfortable and very worried." Then she told him what she had heard.

Jonathon smiled, a soft, gentle smile. "The House Darthar is the oldest house of all of the Feyra houses. When the family broke into two, your side becoming Darthar Na, we still remained a single family. That is also a secret, a family secret." His eyes glittered soft red. "House Darthar and House Darthar Na have remained Shadow Houses, quiet ones who do not appear to be interested in meddling in the affairs of others. All see us as soft retiring and unconcerned. This is a very useful thing to have all those ones think, but it is far from reality." He nodded. "Hofga is correct about messy. Tomorrow we shall visit and see what we shall see."

Morning came, as it always must, and the six sat around a table and enjoyed breakfast. Karanly had joined them.

All through the meal, she had bubbled and teased the three males and her brother, a little. And fed tidbits to Purr Cat who sat next to her chair.

Jonathon stood as all finished their meal and waited for Dee to join him at the door. "Shall we?"

"Let's," she said.

"This is House Adantender."

Dee wondered who their architect had been. The

place looked like a large mound of boulders set in the middle of a boulder field in a rather stark environment.

"Mostly underground," said Jonathon, striding toward a narrow space between two large grey boulders. He knocked on the door.

"Yes?"

"Visitors."

"Who be these visitors?"

"Jonathon and Dee to speak about special skills."

The door opened slowly. "Do come in."

The man waved them inside and gestured toward a door at the end of the short hall. "Come. Please."

In the small, rather comfortable room he served them coffee and sat. A jagged scar curved from his left temple to the tip of his chin.

"What need you to know?" he asked, taking a sip from his cup.

"Capture thing call. Has your house been working with any other?"

"Naz! We keep close and prefer to let others be."

"Good coffee," observed Jonathon. "Do you know of any others with that skill that might work with someone not family?"

The man shrugged. "Comes to that behavior we ask not. Why?"

"Ummm ah," said Jonathon standing. "Many thanks."

"Little said, little done."

Dee stood. "Thank you."

They walked down the hall and outside.

"Next," said Dee.

It was a sprawling structure at the edge of a meadow and a beach. The structure was painted white with blue trim. The beach was very wide and very white.

"Nice place." Dee looked at the setting. "Very pretty."

Jonathon knocked on the door. "House Mbanar."

The door opened, a young woman peered out at them. "Well?"

"We would like to talk about special skills."

"Hun ha." She backed up. "Do come in. Please." Turning away, she led them to a door and into a room with a table and a number of chairs. Picking a coffee pot from somewhere she filled three cups. "You may ask."

Jonathon nodded. "We have no need but wish to know if you ever work with others using a Capture thing call."

She nodded. "House Hasbatan many long ago. Not since." She waggled her free hand. "Many long ago, that time, caused problems, unwanted problems. Never since." She sipped and smiled at him. "Else?"

Jonathon emptied his cup and stood. "Many thanks."

Dee did the same thing. "Many thanks."

The great structure stood in isolation in the vast empty plain.

"House Obiteon," said Jonathon. He stepped over and rapped on the door with the ornate brass door knocker.

"Who?" asked someone.

"Jonathon and Dee."

"What?"

"We would like to discuss special skills."

"When?"

"Now please."

The door slid back and sideways.

"I am Hatil. Do come in." He led them into an alcove and shoved already filled cups at them. "Ask."

"Does your house ever work with others using the Capture thing call." Jonathon sipped. So did Dee.

"Why?"

"A rather minor problem." Jonathon shook his head, jerked, shoved to his feet, and glared around the empty room.

Dee twitched awake.

She was lying in a large bed in a large square room. Sitting up, she looked around. It wasn't one of her rooms. The bed in here was the only furniture, a piece of very heavily built furniture. There were two doors near one corner, one in each wall. The ceiling was very high, making the room a great cube.

The doors appeared to be constructed from

heavy dark timbers, the walls and arched ceiling were grey stone of some sort, smooth and tightly joined.

"Welcome, Daliera," giggled a voice from a wall grill of heavy metal with narrow slits in it. "Heh heh heh. I got you, good and proper."

The voice slurped loudly as the speaker sipped. "Don't try the doors. Bolted from the outside. But don't worry, it is just for four days. You are quite beautiful, you know. And it was very pleasant, for me. But, ummm ah, it would have been ever so much more pleasant if you had participated."

Dee stood, grabbed a bed post to steady herself from a suddenly dizzy head. "What are you talking about? And who are you? And why am I here? And let me out of here!"

"Told you, told you, told you, told you. You are mine and I can do what I want with mine! Well, ah, hum, ummmm, you have been, eh heh, fertilized. Quite unwillingly, rather limp. Can't have you free and loose outside those rooms. Not now. Just won't do!"

"You drugged me and raped me?"

"With a little help from my friends," he laughed. "After all, can't start a new house without offspring now, can I? Oh, don't fret. I will properly reward you. Afterwards. Ummmm ah, well, I will see you later. Four days later, bye bye. Till then. Told you, told you, told you, told you."

"PERVERT!"

She heard the grill cover slide into place. She

walked over and tried the doors. "Latched tight." And looked around. "So this is what a Karthan's room looks like," she mumbled to herself.

She tried a call. But the room was guarded tight.

"OH!" She grabbed her middle and sat heavily on the bed. "Damn fast!"

She lay back and curled up. And thought that it was going to be a long two days.

Some unknown time later she woke and sat up. She felt strange, very strange, and stared at her hands. They were large and her fingers looked much longer than they should. She stood and ran those strange hands over herself. Everything felt strange, very strange. The ceiling was much closer to her head.

"How can I be taller?" She looked down at long muscular legs and heavily clawed feet.

Running her hand over her face she felt two heavy brow ridges. And her face seemed to push further forward, quite a lot further forward. So did her jaw. Her tongue told her that her canines were much longer than they had been before. She could feel them on the outside of her lower lip.

"Damn," she grumbled in a gurgling rasping voice. "So this is what a Karthan feels like." Her stomach growled. She was suddenly very hungry, ravenous. Her mid-section felt thicker, much, much thicker.

Suddenly her stomach muscles clenched and released, over and over and over and over and over.

"AHHHHHHHH!"

More reflex than thought, great hands cupped and caught and cradled the large egg.

Some small corner of her awareness wondered how she could do that.

Then her body heaved and hunched and all that she could think of was the terrible agony. Agony so terrible that the air seemed to turn grey.

Dimly she heard a latch slide free and odors of foot drift into the room through a narrow crack where the door had popped open a small amount.

Then darkness swirled down and around and she knew nothing at all.

She was hunched over the great table eating as fast as she could, slowly reducing that overwhelming hunger.

The outer door popped open and he stepped in, grinning happily. "So, is it a male or a female? AWK!"

Standing on long muscular legs, she held him up, his head just brushing the ceiling, long fingers curled around his neck. Sniffling loudly, head tilted to one side, face close to face, she peered into wide, staring, frightened eyes. He smelled good. She licked her lips, long canines glittering in the soft room light.

Jonathon looked in the door, jumped back, slammed the door, and jammed the heavy bolt into place.

"Dee," said the voice through the wall grill.

"Dee, don't eat him. We need him. We have to talk to him."

She thought about that strange idea. About not eating him. She was called Dee. That was interesting.

Thumping his head against the ceiling until he went limp, she dropping the morsel into a loose heap, and went back to the rest of the better smelling food at the table and began to eat vast quantities.

And finally, she fell asleep in her bed, satiated.

"Dee?" It was a soft voice that she recognized. Her eyes eased open and slowly focused.

Karanly smiled down at her. "Welcome back."

Dee nodded slightly. She was in a bed that seemed to have been torn into shreds.

"You made quite a nest." Karanly helped her sit up. "Jonathon dragged that not nice one to another room. He thinks that he will live long enough."

Karanly gently pulled the shredded material out and away, and gasped.

"What?" Dee jerked.

"TWO! Oh Dee, you have two daughters." Karanly began to laugh and laugh and laugh. She finally gurgled to a stop. "No wonder."

"What? No wonder? What's so funny?"

"That not nice one waited for four days, the normal time, and walked in. But with two eggs, really a rather rare happening, that was one day too early. He was lucky that he wasn't eaten. Like I told you, no one ever gets near Karthan."

She bent and tickled one girl under her chin. "May I carry one? It is time to go home."

Dee crawled from the remains of the bed and wobbled to her feet and pulled on her tattered clothes. "Sure." She carefully lifted the other daughter and headed for the outside hall.

Jonathon walked from a room, a limp body slung over one shoulder. He smiled at Dee.

"Let's go," she rasped.

They ate a late dinner, two young girls sitting on either side of Dee.

"Do they always grow so fast."

"Just a growth spurt. Won't last. It is left over from our primitive days when the newly born had to be able to run with the adults soon after they were born." Karanly smiled at her.

"Where is that guy?"

"Room down the hall," said Jonathon.

"Be right back," said Dee, striding from the room. She was amazed at how fast she had recovered.

She stepped in. Purr Cat was guarding him.

"I want my child!" he snapped at her from his chair.

"Never happen, freak!" She leaned forward and broke his nose with a sharp jab. And straightened up. "I would do more but I think that Jonathon wants to talk to you."

She turned away, then spun back. "However." And kicked him as he stood glowering at her. She watched his eyes fly wide and round as he bent over and gasped. "Hopefully," she said, "that will end your reproductive capabilities." She grinned at him as he stared up at her. "I can always get a knife." She turned and walked back to her dinner.

As they sat sipping coffee, relaxing, Dee in a large couch with her offspring, looking out the large window, Jonathon cleared his throat.

"Ummmmm?" said Dee.

"House Obiteon is a smoking ruin. Ummm, I was rather angry."

She shrugged. "Will that creep tell you anything at all?"

Jonathon nodded. "Everything that he knows."

Karanly grinned at her. "Your daughters will be very pretty. Some time many houses will want to cross-tie."

Jonathon smiled, a soft, gentle smile. "House Darthar Na will startle the families."

Chapter Thirteen

Leaning A Little.

House Darthar Na.

Jonathon walked into the room and sat down. "What happened to you?

"She hit me and kicked me. Don't let her in. She said that she might bring a knife."

Jonathon nodded. "Guess third son's aren't too bright. You didn't treat her very nice."

"She was still a monster. She shouldn't have been."

Jonathon shrugged. "You just miscalculated. Many things." He smiled. "I, ah ummmm, talked with House Obiteon about things."

"I needed her. I wanted her. She is mine!"

"House Obiteon is no more. You can be next. Please explain what you, and what they, were up to and planning?"

Jonathon nodded as he sat down after picking up a cup of coffee from the counter. He sipped.

"It seems that one promised House Obiteon your

second child for their help. Of course, he assumed you would have to be held captive until that could come to pass. He obviously had no idea as what was actually happening. And still doesn't. Nothing else as far as he could babble."

He shrugged and took a sip. "I let him go hobbling across the meadow. I doubt that his house will take him in after they find out what he did. He probably won't survive too long. Houseless Feyra rarely do."

Early the next day as Dee and Jonathon were sitting looking out one of the large windows and sipping coffee, Hofga burst into the room.

"Those hounds wouldn't let me, or any of the others, enter parts of the house. But now they don't seem to mind." He sucked in a deep breath. "I just saw two young girls running down the hall laughing and giggling."

Dee poured a cup and handed it to him. "My daughters." She sat back down.

He dropped into his chair, gulped air and coffee. "Daughters? Your daughters? Two daughters?"

Jonathon nodded. "Just so."

"Hah potah!"

Dee laughed.

He stared at her. "They were running with a great cat-like creature."

"Perfectly safe." Dee sipped.

Jonathon nodded. "Just so."

Hofga held out his cup. "Please?"

She refilled it. "You may always help yourself."

Hofga cleared his throat several times. "Word has come that House Obiteon is no more."

Jonathon nodded. "Yes."

"Jonathon, what is happening?"

He shrugged. "We have much to learn, it seems."

Aranda walked in. Dee stood and handed him a cup and poured. And sat down. "Many thanks," he said. "Word has come that House Panthandar wishes to speak to House Darthar Na about some sort of generational matters."

Dee jumped to her feet and snapped, "There is nothing to discuss! Not now! Not never!" She refilled his cup. Then she looked at Jonathon. "Ah?"

"Yes?"

"Why did that ding bat try to implicate House Farthan?"

Hofga looked at her. "Ding bat?"

"Nut case," she said.

Hofga looked at Jonathon who looked at Dee who stared back at Jonathon, and said, "That not nice one that you let go."

"Ah ummmm." Jonathon nodded at her. At times her people tainted dialect didn't make sense. "Good question. Perhaps he told us more than he thought or knew."

Aranda frowned. "Word is always not nice about that house."

Hofga glared out at the meadow. "Very not nice."

"Bad thought," suggested Jonathon.

"Are there several houses all planning something?" Dee asked.

Hofga, Aranda, and Jonathon stared at her.

Frandel walked in, stopped, looked at the several expressions, and then at the coffee pot. "Bad brew?"

Dee shook her head, stood, and beckoned Jonathon from the room.

As she led him down the room, she asked, "Now what do we do?"

"Very time consuming research. You stay here. It will take days. Until most of the growth spurt of your daughters is done, they need their mother around. Karanly will help and explain. I will be safe. So, you be safe. Here."

He headed for the outside door.

"You sure?" she called.

"Yes. Quite."

She headed up to the third floor where there was an immense training hall. The ceiling had a pair of balconies where the fifth floor doors gained entry to overlooks.

She entered from a third floor door and looked around. Ar was sitting on the floor with her daughters and Purr Cat. All were holding an animated discussion about something.

Karanly popped in and hugged Dee. "Jonathon

suggested strongly that I should visit for awhile."

Dee returned the hug. "Very welcome. Do children always grow that fast?" She gasped, "Oh! I already asked that."

Karanly laughed and hugged her again. They headed over to the small group.

Purr Cat stood and stretched and bumped Karanly with her head.

Karanly stroked one sleek fur covered side. "Wish I had one of these when I was growing up."

Two daughters leaped to their feet and thumped into their mother, laughing happily.

Ar stood and bowed. "Princess."

"Time for a meal," announced Dee. She turned her daughters toward the correct door.

Over the repast Dee heard all about studying hard and that Ar was a stern person who made them pay attention.

"This is Karanly," said Dee.

"I am," said Karanly as she looked at the two young girls, "Karanalador a'Anathor a'Mdator a'Zquar a'Winfa a'Apatin a'Relda d'Darthar, your Damadon." She stood and bowed deeply to each one. "But you should call me Karanly." She bowed to Dee, even deeper. "What the people call Aunt, sort of."

She sat and looked at them.

"I am Tiela, first daughter."

"I am Winala, second daughter."

Moe popped into the room and licked Tiela's ear.

She giggled. "Ar taught us the call, Mother."

Both daughters took more servings from several of the dishes and began to eat. Their growth spurts were burning up lots of energy.

Tiela slipped Moe a sausage while Winala tapped Purr Cat on the tip of her nose with another sausage which was very delicately taken from the holding hand.

Karanly smiled and dumped more food onto her own plate then Dee's. "You need to eat much, also."

Once the meal was finished Ar ushered his two pupils and the two house beasts back to the training hall.

Karanly twisted her chair around and sipped from her cup. "Jonathon is much worried and has gone to visit the Keeper of House Interlinks. It will take him some time to figure out what it is that he thinks he will find. It is a great complicated puzzled, he said."

Jonathon walked into the Archives and told the Keeper what he wished to do and stated that he would be eating his meals here until he was finished.

The Keeper bowed, led him to the appropriate room, and left, assuring Jonathon that all would be as he wished it to be.

Ar walked in and sat at the table with Dee and Karanly.

"Princess, I wish to teach you a new skill. Please

come to the Training Hall.

Karanly nodded. "I will stay here."

After going through the process a dozen times, Ar stepped back five paces. "Now Princess, try it on me. I cannot be hurt."

"You sure?"

"Yes. Most true."

Dee nodded and made a thrusting gesture with her right hand.

Ar was hurtled across the Training Hall and thudded into the wall and bounced to the floor. Slowly he stood, smiled at the two staring young girls, and walked back to Dee.

"Very good, Princess. This is a unique skill of this house. I think that some of your own previous training is coming back. That knowledge was not completely lost it does seem. Ummm ah, this is the third unique skill of House Darthar Na."

He bowed. And nodded at her. "Now do it the other way."

Dee looked at Ar. Ar blew across the hall and crashed into the far wall. Ever so slowly he stood, and walked back to her.

"Are you all right?"

"I am, Princess, I am. But I do need to rest now." He shook his head. "Not a thing for young girls to learn."

Two daughters frowned and said in unison,

"Yes, Ar."

Dee led the pair out a door and down the hall. "Do you know what ice cream is," she asked as they entered the room.

"No, Mother," they said.

Karanly smiled at them and began to serve everyone from a large carton. "It is vanilla."

Damn clever those house sprites, thought Dee, watching her daughters enjoy the treat.

Karanly leaned close to Dee's ear and whispered, "This is pretty good stuff."

"I was hoping for chocolate."

Karanly jerked.

"What? Now?"

"Oh, ah, um," whispered Karanly in Dee's ear. "Our taste buds are different than the people in some things, some flavors. Chocolate is not nice. That is one of your people memories, not us."

"Oh." Dee leaned back. "So, what else is there to know before I serve the wrong thing or ask for the wrong thing to be served."

Karanly grinned at her. "You can't. The house sprites would never do that even if you asked."

Dee sighed. "Will I ever know what I am doing?"

Karanly stood, bent and hugged her. "Sure. It just takes time, that is all." She grinned. "Maybe I will ask Kraz when I am capable again. We could raise offspring together."

"Ah?"

"Yes?"

"Capable again?"

"Oh, that." Karanly tugged her out into the hall. "Offspring are rather young for that discussion."

As they strolled along, arm in arm, Karanly explained that their reproductive systems took a long time to recover before the females could be fertilized again. This is why the families tended to be small and why they treasured their offspring. She laughed. "Of course, you can, ah umm, mess around if you wish."

Then she began to talk and discuss the raising of the young and the correct pacing of their training in the various skills and how the offspring's physical development tended to vary from house to house.

Then she explained how the female line tended to dominate decision making, which is why daughters usually went to the mother's family and the sons to their father's unless the mother or the father relocated to the appropriate family. Sometimes all agreed on a different arrangement.

Karanly smiled. "My mother came to Jonathon's House, so I was raised there. Once I was full grown she relocated back to her house. Kinship lines are very important to us, which is why we have a Keeper of the House Interlinks."

They finished their discussion in a small room with a large outside window and sat and watched night arrive as they chatted and sipped coffee.

They were walking down one of the hallways headed for the Training Hall. It was early morning.

Karanly touched Dee on the shoulder. "I think that third son who captured you and the house that helped him were urged on by those dark ones who are behind whatever it was that was going on. Those ones are trying to keep everything hidden from view by using others."

She jerked to a halt. "Dee, I am worried some for Jonathon. If those ones hear what he is looking into, my brother could be in great danger. That includes you as well."

"What can we do, you and I, one female Feyra and one female Feyra who knows almost nothing about being one of you?"

Dee and Karanly were sitting sipping coffee when Ar walked in. "You called, Princess?"

Dee nodded. "I have something that I want you to do, Ar."

He nodded. "Of course."

"Better sit down," suggested Karanly.

He did and looked puzzled at both of them. "What?"

"Ar," said Dee, sipping. "I want you to talk to our house beasts and ask them to call into the house as many of their kind as will come here. We want to ask a great favor from them."

Ar gasped. "As many as will come? Princess?"

"Yes. The house is large. As many as will come. Please?"

Ar stood. "Most unusual. Most different. Most interesting." He hurried from the room.

Karanly laughed. "Must be your people living. I would never have thought of something like that."

Dee nodded. "If any come. Wonder how long we will have to wait to find out?"

Karanly shrugged. "Your house might get crowded. I called all of Dathar to come here. You are going to meet a whole bunch of relatives. At least those who do come. Not all will, I imagine. Some are very reclusive."

Dee stared at her and frowned. "A whole bunch of relatives?"

Karanly smiled and nodded. "Yes. There are a number of, ah ummm, sub-houses scattered all around." She frowned back at Dee. "Ah ummm, don't look surprised at, umm, oh, some of them. A few of the sub-houses, have gone, ah eh umm, in, emm ah, different directions. Please?"

"Sure." Dee nodded, and began to wonder what on earth Karanly was suggesting this time.

It was two days later and Dee was meeting those that were arriving.

She met two brothers and two sisters of Darthar suta Namel.

Then a man and his mate and their son, who

appeared to Dee to be a teenager walked in, and announced that they were from Darthar suta Ean. Dee wondered how old that apparent teenager really was.

Ar ushered each group to their quarters.

Then Dee met from Darthar suta Zbtan, a woman and her daughter who were followed in by a man, his daughter and her mate who announced grandly that they were House Darthar suta Dundar.

This group went off to a room to discuss some private business between those two sub-Houses.

Ar popped in, after telling that group where they could find their quarters, and announced that the upper floor was being occupied by beasts.

"How many?"

"Other than the resident house beasts," stated Ar, clearing his throat, "there are an additional eight Hounds, four Furleen, and two Tarken. The house beasts are explaining proper house behavior to those others. The house sprites will keep all the doors to that area closed to all visitors other than those you choose to authorize."

He frowned at her.

"Yes?"

"This is beyond my experience. I will not know how to advise you, Princess?"

Dee stood and hugged her surprised Counselor. "We will just have to learn together, Ar. How are my daughters reacting to all this activity?"

He bowed to her. "Very properly, of course. But

with very, very high curiosity."

She laughed and called her daughters as Ar went off to make sure all were getting well settled in their quarters. The trio accompanied by Karanly went to a room to have a meal.

The larger dining rooms were now being utilized for most meals where the conversation was animated as all here caught up on the affairs and activities of sub-families not often visited. All complimented Dee on her daughters. Near twins were a very rare event. All present felt that House Darthar Na had always been considered to be just a bit different, but her having near twins solidified that long held feeling.

Early the next day, six short and wide individuals dressed in thick fur-lined clothes clumped into the room where Dee, Karanly and two daughters were relaxing, looking out a large window and talking softly.

It was two men and two women and one son and one daughter.

Dee thought that they all had very Asiatic features.

Karanly jumped up and introduced them. "Darthar suta Milatan. They heard that you had two daughters, so they brought a pair of Hamal as gifts for them. It is an extremely rare breed which only they can raise. Their House is deep in the Himalaya Mountains."

Dee jumped up and bowed to them, and thanked them for their gift and for coming.

The six grinned wide smiles of gleaming white teeth and bowed low in return. Ar ushered them out and up to their quarters telling them that clothing suitable for the local climate would be waiting for them there.

Two daughters stared at their mother with wide eyes.

Dee laughed. "Shall we go see what they are?"

Four very curious individuals headed up to see what the gifts looked like.

"Wow!" Dee looked at Karanly. "Really white! They sorta look like very sleek polar bears except their faces are more cat-like than bear-like."

Karanly smiled at the daughters.

The Hamal walked over to sniff at the young girls, their movements and manner much more feline than ursine. They had been told to each pick a young girl to protect.

"They are beautiful," said Tiela, running her hand over the thick white fur.

Really are," agreed Winala, doing the same thing.

Dee leaned close to Karanly and whispered, "Will the hounds get jealous?"

"They know better," she whispered back.

Purr Cat flowed over to them followed by four other Furleen. She bumped the two Hamal with her head and warbled to them, for some time. Then with a twitch of her tail, the Furleen pack left.

The Hamal chirped at the young girls and then each bumped their chosen daughter with their head.

Karanly laughed. "Looks like two daughters have very special guardians."

"Bed time," announced Dee, who received two kisses, and then watched the four head for the bedroom.

"They are going to be well guarded," said Karanly.

"Even if they make them into pets?"

"Especially if they make them into pets. Good night, Dee, sleep well."

Three days later Karanly introduced a woman and her two daughters to Dee and winked at her. "Another rare happening."

The trio were from Dathar suta Ocedaron. The woman was over six feet tall with the daughters showing signs of being as tall or taller.

Karanly ushered them to their bedroom and returned. "They like water," she said to Dee. "And being in the water."

Later, in the large dining room, Dee looked at them all. A number of soft discussions were going on in different small groupings as members of the sub-houses caught each up on events, major or minor. The younger members had self segregated and held more animated discussions, showing greater curiosity about their relatives, less restraint in their movements, and more laughter.

The adults kept a careful but discrete watch for bad manners or inappropriate questions.

Dee leaned sideways and spoke ever so softly to Karanly. "Have you hear from Jonathon. He has been gone for a long time."

Karanly smiled. "A very short time. He must be all right. We would hear otherwise."

After dinner all scattered in small clusters to sit in various of the rooms and sip coffee and talk quietly.

Dee, Karanly, and two daughters did the same.

The light outside was fading when they walked in: three men, three women, three daughters, and two sons.

Karanly laughed. "The rest of House Dathar has arrived." She stood, so did Dee.

The group bowed deeply in unison.

"Sister," said the older looking of the men.

"Jant," said Karanly. "This is Dee. Dee, Jant is the second brother." Then she named each of the others and their birth rank. Ar appeared and led them away, asking as the door closed whether they would like a meal first.

Jonathon stuffed all the pages of his notes inside his shirt and ran, from the room, down the hallway, and through the outside door of the House of Interlink

Records, and into the darkness, fading from sight.

The ground all around the large building was ripped and torn, all the nearby trees shredded into splinters. Great things still prowled and grumbled here and there.

Suddenly they were gone as someone howled anger when they realized that their victim, some nosy unknown, had somehow fled the building and past the watching things.

In the distance an large shape coasted on silent wings just above the forest top, down the valley, and out into the surrounding countryside.

The moon was flooding her bedroom with silver silence as the middle of night eased ever so slowly toward dawn and a new day.

He crashed in, rolling and thumping to thud heavily against one wall.

Lights popped on as Dee leaped to her feet and crouched, glaring at whoever or whatever lay there breathing heavily.

Purr Cat oozed silent threat toward it, belly close to the floor, ears laid back.

Slowly the intruder stood, shimmered, and rasped, "Can I get a cup of coffee, Dee?"

"Jonathon, what happened? You are a mess?" Purr Cat sat and stared at him.

Tiela and Winala stood on the bed and stared at him, their Ice Cats gurgling deep in their throats, the hair on their backs rippling up and down their spines, the warning gesture of the Hamal.

Dee helped him stand and led him to the door. "Back to bed, back to sleep, all of you!" she ordered. "This way," she said to him. "A small comfortable room with comfortable chairs."

Inside the room he fell into a chair and took the filled cup from her hand and took a sip. "Ahhhhh! Very nice." He smiled at her. "How did you get those?"

"A gift from Milaton for the girls. You want a meal? You look tired, and, ummmm, very dirty."

"Umm ah, a meal would be good, then a bath, and the sleep, lots of sleep. House filling up?"

She shrugged. "I really have no idea how big this place really is or how many visitors it can really hold. Of any kind." She refilled his cup, and topped up her own.

He took a sip. "Kind?"

She grinned. "We have lots more house beasts. Don't be surprised if you see packs of them walking here and there. Ar is keeping track of them, I hope." She looked at him.

"What?"

"Exactly how large is the family. So far six subhouses have turned up as well as your house. None of the groups are very large, in numbers, are they?"

"Ummm ah, no. Not any longer."

"Huh?"

"Once upon a long time ago our numbers were

much greater. It is why this house and most of the others are so large because of all the visiting back and forth. But the people expanded so rapidly we had to shrink and to hide, so to speak. And we reproduce so slowly as an adaptation to our elongated life spans that we have to be careful. There are still many places left where we can stay out of sight. But the people technology is getting to be a big problem for us."

He yawned widely. And stood. "Time to sleep, Dee. Sorry that I woke you and all that."

She nodded to him as he left the room and then headed back to her bedroom and found two daughters and two Ice Cats sprawling in her bed. After some shoving of two inert bodies around and telling the grumbling pets to get down, she found a spot between her daughters and fell asleep, wondering what Jonathon had learned.

Chapter Fourteen

Unwinding A Web.

House Darthar Na.

The morning sun shown into the small room where Dee and Jonathon sat. Dee's daughters and Karanly had gone off to visit the house beasts whose number had increased yet again. There were now an additional four Furleen, four Hounds, two Tarken, and six Kartan, the strange grizzly bear shaped beasts with the large and thick scales.

"Dee, it is as twisted a web as I have ever seen. Your parents were correct. It is a dark thing that has been a long time building. I can understand now why they took you out into the world of the people to hide their only offspring. And I am sure that dark is what killed them."

He sipped at his coffee and looked over the cup at her. "If that third son hadn't interfered they would have probably killed you as well. So, in a very strange way, he saved your life even if it is not what he meant to do."

She frowned. "Ugly way to be saved."

He held out his cup. She filled it. He nodded. "Your daughters are lovely."

She laughed. "Growing like weeds."

"Not much longer. Then the real growing begins." He tapped his forehead. "In here. They have so much to learn."

"Like me."

He nodded and smiled, a soft, gentle smile. "Yes. Are all the relatives behaving themselves?"

"Far as I can tell."

"Daughters like their Ice Cats?"

"Absolutely. It is like having four children, only two of them are covered in white fur."

"And how are you doing?"

"Fine. Now I know three special skills. Do you have any idea how many there are?"

He shrugged. "Every house is different. Each house went in unique directions that way."

"And you?" She sipped. "How many? Skills?"

"Ah umm eh." He shrugged. "I, um, ah, lost track. Let's just say, many many."

She stared at him.

"Each house is different."

Dee nodded. "O.K."

Jonathon waggled one hand, the one not holding his cup. "Karanly has different skills. She is female."

Dee sat upright. "So if I had a son he would learn different things that I am or my daughters are learning?"

He nodded. "Most likely. I have no way to know that. The houses do not share that kind of knowledge. But it is the usual pattern."

"Ahhhh." She sipped. "Now what?"

"Ummmmm?"

"Do we do? About this dark web plot or whatever it is?"

"Travel silently. Ask carefully. Some family is at the center. That is what we need to know. Who, which house that is. This thing must be stopped."

"Sure. When do we start?"

"Next day. May we, you and I, visit your daughters?"

"Of course." She stood. "Let's go."

In the Training Hall they stood and watched.

Dee smiled. He gasped.

Tiela and Winala were coasting, in great wide circles, around the hall, wings pumping just enough to do that. The Ice Cats were thumping along after them.

"Beautiful," said Dee. "Two angels."

"They can't be seen, Dee. It would start a wild religious fervor among the people."

"I suppose."

"What else can they do? If I may ask?"

"Ar taught them call. I think that the house beasts adopted them, or maybe it is the other way around." She grinned. "Not many children have pets like that."

He nodded. "I am going to talk with Hofga." He left the training hall.

Dee launched into the air and coasted up behind her daughters. "You too have to be careful. I ran into a wall when I started."

Tiela laughed and Winala giggled as the trio tilted around a corner.

"And do not wear out the Ice Cats. They are still young."

"Oh," said Winala, dropping to the floor, her wings disappearing, and hugging one of the Ice Cats.

Tiela landed next to the other one and did the same thing.

Dee thumped down next to Ar. "They behaving?"

He bowed deeply. "For young ladies!"

Dee laughed. "Yes, I suppose so. I am leaving tomorrow to help Jonathon."

Ar jerked. He ran over to his students and told them to go get something to eat. As soon as they left, he ordered all the doors locked. And walked back. "Time for your next lesson, Princess."

After breakfast, Dee said goodbye to her daughters and walked with Jonathon to the outside. "O.K.," she said. "Let's go."

The park was large and surrounded with tall structures. They stepped from the tight circle of trees and looked around. Jonathon pointed at one of the buildings.

"New York, New York," sang Dee. "What'a town."

Jonathon stopped at the door to a building. "Umm ah."

"What?"

"We need information that they may not want to give."

"And?"

"I intend to get it."

"Oh, oh."

"Yesss."

"Let's go."

They rode the elevator up to the penthouse.

"This is House Filna. We are starting with the least houses. Ready?"

"Sho nuf."

"What?"

"Yes."

Jonathon knocked on the door and thought that she had certainly acquired some strange language from living as one of the people.

The door opened and a young appearing male looked out at them. He was dressed in robes of a soft red.

"Yes?"

"We wish to talk," said Jonathon. "With you."

The door was slammed shut and locked.

Jonathon frowned at the door and sighed. "Step sideways, Dee."

She did. He struck the door.

The force of his blow hurtled lots of things into the room, including pieces of the door and the surrounding structure.

Jonathon leaped inside, grabbed the staggering young man by the throat and lifted him from the floor.

"We wish to talk. With you. Will you do that? Nod, if you will."

He nodded and thumped to the floor.

"Who are you?" he rasped, rubbing his throat.

"Should have brought Karanly along. She does heal." Jonathon pointed at a chair. "SIT!" Dee nodded.

Karanly popped in. "Who did that to the door?"

"I did." Jonathon pointed at the young man. "He has a sore throat."

"Poor dear." Karanly bent and touched his neck. "There you are. Nice robes."

Jonathon nodded at Dee. "Thanks." He whirled around and glared at the seated figure. "Shall we talk? Now?"

"I will."

"I am Jonathon. And this is what I wish to know." He told him. "Now we will discuss other matters."

Dee sat next to Karanly who whispered, "He better help. Jonathon is very unhappy about what he found out."

The soft conversation went on and on with Jonathon taking a note now and then, sometime nodding at what he was told. Finally they were done. Jonathon put his notes away and sat back.

"Now will you give me your true promise that you will not say or do anything with or to anyone or anything about anything that we have discussed here? Yes?"

He nodded.

"Say it!"

"True promise. I do so swear."

"Good choice." Jonathon stood. "Let's go. I am hungry. I saw a restaurant downstairs."

The trio walked through the debris to the elevator and rode down to the restaurant level.

"Pretty good," said Karanly, sipping from her coffee cup.

"Greek," said Dee.

Jonathon took another helping.

"So?" said Dee.

"What?"

"Did you find out?"

"Ah," replied Jonathon. "Not much. He merely made what I had suspected a little more clear."

"Tell us."

He nodded. She refilled his coffee cup.

"It seems that there really is a sort of political thing, a dark gathering to, ah ummmm, become rulers, of a sort, over all the houses. This, umm, group believes that with sufficient numbers of houses gathered together, gathering in power, that they will be able to make all do their bidding."

She refilled his cup. "So they would be dictators, is that it?"

"Of a sort. They think that we, the Feyra, have been hidden too long for too much of the people time, and that we should now claim our own, ummm, position in the affairs of the people."

"A seat on the U.N.?"

"No. They think that we should tell the people, ah, how to behave."

"That sounds really dumb to me. No one would agree to that."

"I know." Jonathon looked at her. "Dee, that dark group just does not want to understand. We may be able to do things that the people can't and all that. But we can't prevent what the people technology can do."

Dee waved over a waiter and ordered vanilla ice cream and more coffee and watched him hurry away.

"So, what do we do?"

"Stop them. No other way."

"Oh, my." Karanly stared at her brother.

"Small carnage instead of extinction." Jonathon sipped at his coffee and sighed. "Zealots are always so tiring."

Dee set her hand on top of his. "I'll help. I agree.

Besides, payback is a bitch. They killed my parents. They need to pay for that, if for nothing else."

Karanly nodded.

Dee looked at him. "What happens if red robe upstairs doesn't stick to his promise?"

Karanly gasped. "Break a true promise?"

"Uh huh."

"Not nice," said Jonathon standing, setting a pile of money on the bill, and heading for the outside door.

He led them back into the park over to the correct cluster of trees. As they stepped inside the grove, the sky glowed in a bright flash of red.

"He didn't keep his promise," said Jonathon, taking them away.

Dark anger swirled around him in billows as he stormed in and around the chairs of those gathered in this place. Finally, he stopped and glared at the ones assembled.

"House Filna," he growled, "is no more."

"What?" asked one of them.

"House Filna is vanished."

"A minor house," someone suggested.

"One less house to aid us!" he snapped. "Do any of you know what happened?"

A sea of blank faces looked back.

"I WANT TO KNOW," he screeched. "I WANT YOU TO FIND OUT WHAT HAPPENED TO THEM!" he bellowed. "I WANT TO KNOW WHY!" he howled.

They rushed from the room.

Some few days later they gathered.

"So?" he asked.

"The people fire department claims that it was an accidental gas explosion," said one.

"The people police department of that city issued a report saying the same thing," added another one.

"Of course," he grumbled, shaking his head.

"We," he said, pointing at those gathered, "must be sure that those reports are correct and that it was that and nothing more. I want all to ask careful for anything else." He dropped into his chair.

"DO IT! GO!"

The room emptied in a rush.

"House Tatarnon." Jonathon pointed at the many spires poking above the tree tops not too far into the forest from where they stood. "They are also on the edge of that dark thing. Shall we speak with them?"

"Sure."

"Of course," agreed Karanly.

They walked along, following the narrow path that wandered in and out and around the trees until they stood before the door.

Jonathon rapped on the polished metal.

The door swung in and she looked out at them. "Yes?"

"We wish to talk," said Jonathon.

"Do come in." She stepped back, becking them to follow her into a small room with a table having four chairs and four cups already filled.

"Your arrival was noted." She sat and took a sip from her coffee. "What?"

Jonathon carefully explained.

"Oh. Most clever of you." She stood and snatched a weapon from somewhere.

The ice blast snapped through her chest hurtling the body back into the wall. It thumped into a loose heap on the floor and leaked dark fluids across the polished wood.

Karanly stared at Dee's still extended finger. "Dee?"

"Ar thought that I might need something like this." She swallowed hard. "But he didn't have time to explain much nor did we have much time to practice."

Karanly handed her a filled cup. "Here. You look a little pale."

Jonathon stood, looked at them, and turned for the door. "We have to talk with another member of the family. Wait here." He walked out and away.

And in just a brief moment returned with a young woman, his hand clamped around her upper left arm. "A daughter."

Dee stood."Please sit." She nodded at the lump and the mess on the floor. "We really didn't want to do something like that but she tried to kill us."

Jonathon released the daughter, walked over and

picked something from the floor. "A slay wand. A very rare construction skill. Your house?"

The young woman shook her head. "No! She was forced to take that thing. We had no choice. It was join or die. She was much afraid." She sat and stared from face to face, tears pouring down her cheeks. "Help us. They will kill us now."

"Who forced you?" asked Jonathon.

"House Zertanor. We cross-tie three back."

"Umm ah."

"Please?" she said. "Now it is just my younger brother and me."

Jonathon nodded. And said something soft to Dee.

He appeared, eyes darting from face to face. "Brother?"

Jonathon nodded and looked at her.

"Nerela," she said.

"Nerela, this is Jant, second brother. Jant, this is Nerela, new Head of House Tatarnon. She and her younger brother are to be protected. Do whatever you feel is best."

Jant bowed to Nerela. "Princess, I will see that it is so."

Jonathon stood and beckoned Dee and Karanly from the room. "Jant will do just as he said. Shall we proceed?"

They went to Dee's house.

Jonathon persuaded her that they ought to spend a few days or so resting, relaxing, and visiting. And to wait and see whether anyone would react to what had happened so far.

Jonathon and Dee were by themselves finishing breakfast on the third day when someone knocked ever so politely on their door.

"Come in," called Dee.

Jant walked in followed by Nerela. Both bowed deeply.

"Princess," said Jant. "Nerela has agreed to my, umm ah, proposal. So , ah umm, we came here to, um eh, visit with Jonathon and you."

Dee poured two additonal cups full and waved them to empty chairs.

"What?" asked Jonathon, leaning back and taking a sip.

Jant bowed to his older brother. "I am leaving the house and joining with Nerela. Her brother does agree. How say you to this?"

Jonathon smiled and looked at Dee who nodded.

"Stay here with your brother," said Dee to Nerela. "It is safer."

Jonathon stood and bowed to Jant and to Nerela. "We give welcome to House Tatarnon. How did she enter?"

Ar stepped into the room. "I allowed it. It seemed, um ah, the thing to do. And the younger male as well."

Dee winked at Ar and asked them all, "Is there some special ceremony for this?"

Karanly danced into the room, laughing. She hugged Jant and then Nerela. "Certainly is. It will be the biggest in ever so long as we have most of the House gathered here."

Dee looked at Ar who stated, "We have a grand hall which is large enough. Princess?"

"Sure," said Dee.

"Tomorrow," said Ar, turning and heading out the door. Two young girls darted in followed by two Ice Cats.

"My daughters," said Dee to Nerela. "Tiela and Winala, and their pets."

Nerela carefully watched the Ice Cats as Dee was hugged from either side.

"Ar told us," said Tiela.

"That there will be a great cross-tie ceremony," continued Winala.

"Tomorrow," finished Tiela.

Dee laughed and indicated the other two. "This is Jant and Nerela. Of House Tatarnon." She pointed at two chairs. "Sit. Join us."

He banged the table with his fist hard enough that the table made cracking sounds.

"House Tatarnon had withdrawn from our plan. Someone go there and destroyed them and their dwelling. This just can not be allowed."

"A minor house," some mumbled.

A bony finger jabbed at the speaker. "Then House Pintar will do the deed."

The mumbler stood and stomped from the room.

"Anyone have any idea?" he snarled.

As they shook their heads he ordered them from the room.

The members of House Pintar stood in front of House Tatarnon and talked softly. Then the Head stepped up and banged on the door. And waited. And then he did it again.

Finally he stopped, his hand was throbbing. He looked at his brother and sister. "Join with me. This structure must come down."

They ordered in dark things that thrashed and pummeled and tore and wrenched at the building and then howled in frustration at the lack of results.

"Heavily warded," observed the brother.

"Strangely so," added the sister.

Nine Furleen charged them from nine directions.

House Pintar was scattered over the grass and the outer wall of House Tatarnon.

The Furleen sat, licked their fur clean, and then flowed feather soft into the surrounding forest.

The great cross-tie ceremony had ended and the celebration was rapidly shifting toward the boisterous.

The males who were considered old enough

were passing around great mugs and beginning to look a little glazed in the eye. The females had formed a cluster around Nerela and were talking softly, keeping one eye on their house males, and giving her small gifts.

Ar walked up to Dee, whispered in her ear, and led her to a quiet room.

Purr Cat flowed from the wall and sat in front of her, and licked a few specks from one paw, and told her.

Dee gasped. "I will tell Jonathon. Please thank all of your clan for us."

"Thank you, Princess." Purr Cat slipped from the room.

"My," said Dee.

"Truly a surprise," stated Ar.

"Really?"

"Indeed. I had no idea that they would do things like that so, ummm, independently."

"Learn something new all the time. I will tell Jonathon tomorrow. I think that the guys are probably not in good shape right now for that kind of talk." She walked from the room and went to see what the females were up to.

Dark scowled ugly in all directions as he howled at them, "I WANT TO KNOW WHY!"

One of them had reported that House Pitar was quiet, apparently empty, and that no trace of them had been found. And that House Tatarnon was untouched and had, in fact, joined in the second brother of House Darthar to the first daughter of House Tatarnon, now Head of that house.

He sizzled. "House Darthar? Are you sure?"

"Absolutely."

"I wonder," he grumbled at them all.

"Most of House Darthar is gathered in House Darthar Na for the cross-tie ceremony so word said."

"Yesssss. Word did say that the only daughter had become Head of House Darthar Na and had caused some problem for House Parthandar. Can any gathered here explain what that problem might have been?"

The usual blank faces peered up at him.

"Perhaps some enterprising member could go and find out? GO!"

They scattered in all directions.

Dee ate a late breakfast with Jonathon and Karanly. "That was quite a celebration. Is it always like that?"

He carefully shook his head.

Karanly grinned at him. "Most of the family gathered together like that is a rare event." She refilled their cups. "Maybe it shouldn't be like that. I think that it would be good for the families to gather together more often."

He carefully nodded. And sipped from his cup. And croaked, "You may plan that. We are not traveling until tomorrow."

Ar appeared and bowed to them all, looked at Dee, and beckoned her from the room.

Outside, in the hall, she asked, "Yes?"

"Two more Tarken have arrived as have two more Kartar."

"Do we still have room?"

"Of course. Although they now occupy most of that floor."

"And?" She laughed. "I can tell from the expression on your face."

He cleared his throat. "Word has come that House Amada and House Omptar are asking about House Parthandar and House Darthar Na behaviors."

"Ummmmm."

"Indeed, Princess, indeed."

"Will this be a problem? Of some sort?"

"Hard to say."

Dee nodded. "O.K., thanks" She went back in to join Jonathon and Karanly.

They made their report.

He stared at them. "WHAT!"

The Head of House Omptar cleared his throat. "It seems, as we just told, that the third son of House Parthandar, aided by the now extinct and destroyed House Obiteon, captured and forcefully fertilized the Head of House Darthar Na."

He shook his head. "Unheard of!"

The Head of House Amada cleared his throat.

"Most true. Ahem, ahem, she birthed. The third son seems to be either lost or dead, and House Obiteon, as you just heard, is nothing but ruins. And House Darthar Na refuses to speak with House Parthandar."

He stared at them. "Surely this female is not that powerful. Her parents died."

"Word is that she was helped by, ah umm, someone or something. Nothing seems to know who or what."

"Who or what?"

The Head of House Amada nodded. "House Darthar Na was known in the always past to collect and keep rare wild beasts in their dwelling. Perhaps something came to her rescue."

He nodded. "Perhaps. That house was always a quiet house, not interested in being bothered. Ah well."

Jonathon stood in front of the Gathering Hall and addressed all the Heads about what he had found out so far. "That dark plan should not be allowed. I wish all to discuss among themselves what they wish to do. Dee and I are leaving to visit another of the minor houses of this black gathering. Maybe this time it will not be so bad."

He and Dee headed from the room and down the hall. "Let us hope so," he said.

She stared at it. "What a cute cottage. Cute and small."

Jonathon smiled, a soft, quiet smile. He pointed at it. "Not as small as it seems. House Gilana is noted for illusion skills."

He knocked on the door.

It swung open. A man and a woman beckoned them in. "Do come in." And led them down a high ceiling hall and into a room with comfortable chairs. They filled cups and handed them to Dee and Jonathon, then sat, facing the pair.

"So, Jonathon," said the man.

"We wondered," said the woman.

Jonathon nodded. "How did this house get involved in such dark?"

The man reached over and held her hand. "We had no choice. We have yet to have offspring. House Canatal said that we would never live that long if we did not help those. No choice, no choice."

Jonathon nodded. And spoke softly to Dee.

He appeared and bowed deeply. "Brother?"

"This," said Jonathon, "is third brother Hakar. He will over layer wards on your house if you true promise to sever from this dark."

The pair stood and bowed deeply to Hakar, Jonathon, and Dee.

"True promise," said the man.

"True promise," said the woman.

"And great debt to House Darthar and to House Darthar Na," the man added.

"However we may do that," she added.

Hakar nodded to Jonathon. "This house will be safe."

"Yes." Jonathon nodded back, and turned to Dee who followed him from the room.

"HOUSE GILANA DID WHAT?"

Black billowed outward, bouncing from the walls and ceiling.

The Head of House Zilan bowed and mumbled, "As I did just now say. They pulled away from us."

"That miserable puny house would dare that?"

"Most so."

"Go remove it. And send word around as to why they are no more." It was time to make people understand that they would do what they were told.

"At once."

Jonathon knocked on the door set in the high, rose colored, stone wall of House Canatal and glared at it.

"Jonathon?"

"I do not like high houses doing what they did. We had enough of that many long ago. I thought that one understood that!" He banged on the door. "Open!"

The door parted down the middle as both halves swung inward.

"Yes," said the man.

"We came to talk."

"About?"

"House Gilana."

"Ah umm ah."

"Exactly."

"Perhaps we do not wish to discuss that matter."

"We came to talk."

He stepped back. "Do come in."

They followed him into a room that was all stone and stark. He waved at the chairs. "Sit."

"Canatal charm," growled Jonathon.

"Why worry you on House Gilana?"

"Why does a high house do such napata?"

"COARSE!" The man leaped to his feet and pointed. "Not welcome! Go!"

Jonathon sat and looked at him. "Why?"

The man glared at him. "Not to be talked about! Not to be shared! Not to be stopped!"

"Ah ummm," said Jonathon.

The ceiling in a far corner fell into the room.

"Poor construction," suggested Jonathon. "Poor judgement." More ceiling fell. "Poor taste in friends." One wall bowed outward.

"STOP THAT!"

"Ah ummm." Jonathon stood and took Dee's arm. "Might as well leave."

"Never return!" shouted the man as he slammed the outer door.

"No need." Jonathon led Dee down the narrow path and around the first bend. And took them out.

The room shuddered, dust drifted down from the cracks forming in the ceiling. Black angry poured out.

"What!"

The Head of House Zilan nodded. "Oh do stop doing that!" His house was equal to the speaker's.

"You dare?"

He nodded. "House Gilana is warded many layers deep by someone else. Nothing may affect it." He jabbed a finger at the glaring man. "So think. What house can do that?"

A member of their group ran into the room. "House Canatal collapsed! A heap of rubble. No survivors."

"And who can do that?" asked the Head of House Zilan. "Stop gushing black! It is time to think. We are slowly coming apart. Minor houses are minor and offered little. But House Canatal was not minor!"

He poured a cup of coffee and sat and sipped. And was glared at for doing that. He poured another cup and shoved it across the table. "Here, poor host, have a cup of coffee."

"Someone is meddling."

"Does seem so."

"Who would dare?"

"Very few, very few."

He glared at the one that had rushed in. "Go! Send those who are most able to visit those few and ask."

Dee, two daughters, Jonathon, and Karanly had finished breakfast and were relaxing, sipping coffee.

She walked in. A tall female dressed all in silver colored clothes. Her hair was white as white can be.

Karanly smiled at her. "Second sister, Silneana. Welcome."

She sat. Dee filled a cup for her.

Silneana sipped, then said to Jonathon, "The Heads of House Abalam, Untervale, and Trillmar wish to visit with you. They wait outside the door."

Dee and Jonathon hurried to the outside door and Dee beckoned them inside. "Do come in."

She led them to a small room sit with a table, chairs, cups, and steaming pots of coffee.

The oldest of them bowed to her. "I am Daros, Head of House Untervale." He sat. Dee filled his cup.

The woman bowed to her. "Guindar, Head, House Trillmar." She sat. Dee filled her cup.

The last bowed to her. "I am Agarant, Head of House Abalam." The man sat. Dee filled his cup.

Jonathon waited until they were very settled and had taken a sip or two.

"Three high houses," stated Jonathon, mostly for Dee's benefit. "Of what do you wish to discuss?"

All looked at Agarant.

He nodded. "We have all been visited and asked questions, very pointed questions, very impolite, pointed questions. Afterwards we gathered and discussed and decided that you should know of this."

"Ummm ah," said Jonathon.

"We, ah um ah, made subtle seek know and do feel, we do, that those three high houses with the impolite questions are involved in forbidden dark."

Jonathon nodded. And sipped.

"We will tell you the names. If House Darthar wishes it to be so, we will aid and support however we might."

"Most generous." Jonathon stood and bowed to each of them. "Most." He looked at Dee.

She stood and bowed to each of them. "Very kind." And sat.

Agarant nodded. "Preventing whatever it is, is in our own interests. We feel, we do, that our interests are also those of House Darthar. Be this so?"

"Indeed," said Jonathon.

Agarant handed him a piece of paper. "These are the house's names. Do as you wish." He nodded at Dee, than at Jonathon. "Careful, most careful."

Jonathon nodded.

Dee smiled at them. "You may, if you wish, stay and visit with all gathered in."

The three stood and bowed to her.

"Most gracious," said Agarant. "However, we all have houses to see to and plans to make."

The trio left the room.

"Three high houses up to dark matters." Jonathon compared the names on the piece of paper with the names on his chart. "They should know better." He nodded at her. "We will visit the lessor of the three. And see what we shall see, learn what we shall learn."

Dee nodded. "Tomorrow."

"Yes."

He glared at them. "What!"

"As we said, the three high houses all claimed no knowledge of any house, high or minor, with that particular skill, ummm, to be able to collapse great stone structures."

"And these same three high houses have refused our overtures and are not interested in our most noble goal?"

"Just so."

"Would anyone talk with House Darthar?"

The three violently shook their heads.

"Not now," said one.

"Why is that?"

"That house is in the middle of a great ingather at House Darthar Na. Such a gathering might, umm ah, tend toward the, ah umm, unruly if they felt badly disturbed or bothered or even insulted by sharp questions or discussion."

He nodded.

He looked at the three. "Perhaps some lower house?"

They nodded and left.

He wondered why it was so hard to get what

they wanted to happen, to happen. It was, after all, a most noble goal.

Jonathon pointed at the large structure among the many large structures along this street. "High house Pineta. The least of the three we were told. Who would notice them in this setting."

He stepped up to the door and knocked. "They were always known to be careful conservative. Why would they change?"

The door opened.

"Greetings, Dudar, we came to speak."

"You," gasped Dudar.

Jonathon nodded. And waited.

"Do . . . come, do come in," rasped Dudar.

They entered a wide high ceiling grand hall, all ornate woods and carved paneling, hung with great portraits.

"Wowie," said Dee. "Quite a place."

Dudar stared at her.

"This is Dee, Hard of House Darthar Na," explained Jonathon. He pointed at a door. "In there, I believe." And walked through that doorway and into the room.

Dudar and Dee hurried after him.

Plush chairs were set around a great fire place with lighting bathing everything in soft gold light.

Jonathon sat in one chair and waved them grandly into two others.

Dee sat and watched the startled Dudar sit. His eyes darted from her's to Jonathon's.

"What?" asked Dudar. "What do you want? Here? Jonathon?"

"Just a small conversation between long time aquaintences."

"Ummm."

"Yes."

Dee watched carefully.

Jonathon leaned back. "Dudar, what have you entangled yourself with? This time? You agitated House Abalam with poor manners and impolite questions." He steepled his fingers just under his chin. "Tell me, do."

Dudar shifted one way then the other. "Jonathon?"

"Please?"

Dudar exhaled loudly and slumped. "It sounded so correct at the time. The Feyra have been here long before the people were even small groups just surviving. Now what are we? The invisible folk. What are we? Those who are ever so careful to have none of them know that we exist." He slumped deeper.

Jonathon nodded. "So some proposed we should take our proper and rightful place in their communities? And them tell them how to behave, etc., etc., etc.?"

Dudar nodded.

Jonathon jerked upright. Dudar twitched violently. Jonathon glared at him. "Is your group deliberately stupid?"

"No!"

"Do you realize, Dudar, how few of us there really are, world wide? And how many of them there are, world wide? Have you paid any attention at all as to how they react when they feel threatened? Do you really think that three or four hundred Feyra could withstand billions of people intend on doing not nice things to us with their terrible technology?"

"Ummm."

"Think, Dudar, think! For once in a very long life, think!" Jonathon waggled one hand and snarled, "Someone in your group frightened her parents into doing a desperate thing, doing desperate behaviors, and then killed them. And she was the only child!"

Jonathon surged to his feet. "Should someone do that to House Pineta, make your son an orphan?"

Dudar shook his head violently. "NO!"

"Then." Jonathon dropped back into his chair. "Then leave this dark group before that comes true. This house is strong. You can survive. I will help."

He glared at Dudar. "But think on this. I am not interested in having to go hide in cracks and crannies and crevices while hordes hunt and kill Feyra because ignorant egos frightened the people into terror for us all."

Jonathon settled himself, sucked in a deep breath, and whispered, "Do you understand?"

"Yes . . . yes, I do." Dudar looked up through his eyebrows at his friend. "Believe me, please. I really do."

"HOUSE PINETA PULLED OUT!" he howled at the them.

"THEY DARED TO DO THAT!" he bellowed at the startled faces.

"KILL THEM!" he snarled.

"Not possible," said someone.

"Spineless, spineless, spineless," he chanted, stomping back and forth.

He stopped and glared at the assembled group. "Someone is meddling. Dudar in not that intelligent. I want to know who is meddling. And why they are meddling. And see if there any other houses that have similar skills to Pineta!"

They ran from the room. And some began to wonder whether this was really such a good idea. And some began to puzzle about the behavior that they had been seeing. And some began to question, very silently to themselves, the entire concept that they were pursuing. None was willing to express what they were thinking out loud.

Jonathon sat with Dee in a small room after evening meal and watched the moon rise.

"Dudar is not a very deep thinker. He is very talented in his house skills but he does tend to follow without asking if it is presented in just the way that he would accept." He nodded at Dee. "His son will do much better when he becomes the head."

Tiela and Winala carried in trays with bowls and

containers of vanilla ice cream followed by the Ice Cats.

"Ar said that you were in here," explained Tiela as Winala handed around the bowls and the spoons.

They stood in the town square and looked at the hill not all that far away. The top of that hill was covered by a sprawling structure.

"It looks like Medieval castle," said Dee.

Jonathon nodded. "It was built about that period of time as the people figure around an even earlier building that was on the site. That is House Omptar. They have always thought too much of themselves. I think that they would be tempted greatly to be at the head of something dark that satisfied over-blown egos."

He stared at the ornate structure and sipped from his cup. They had bought coffee in the nearby shop. "Dee," he sighed, "this is not how you should be learning about us, about yourself."

She nodded and jabbed him gently in the ribs with an elbow. "I really enjoyed meeting all the relations that I have met so far and I am learning a lot from Ar."

She laughed at his expression. "For someone who grew up an only child and alone and thought that she was one of the people, I never realized what I missed, or was missing."

She waved her free arm at the castle. "Well, let's go up there and see what they have to say." She grabbed his arm as he started forward. "Are they going to try something, ah, not nice?"

"They might."

"Um, O.K., let's go."

They ambled around the square, bought something to eat from a street vender and then headed up the road toward the hill top, just two tourists among the many. Until they passed through the great gate and into the castle grounds proper.

She looked around at the empty space.

Jonathon smiled, a soft, gentle smile. "We see the gate. The people do not. They see a small opening telling them that the castle is closed to visitors. No one noticed us go inside. I watched."

They crossed the close cropped grass and stepped up to the door.

"Ready?"

"As I ever will be," said Dee, suddenly surrounded by Furleen who quickly faded into the castle surface.

Jonathon nodded and thumped on the door.

The door swung in on rust creaking hinges.

In the dim interior they could just barely see the figure standing there.

"We would like to talk," said Jonathon.

Dee smiled.

A deep voice asked, "About what?"

Jonathon frowned at the speaker. "Problematic behavior and dying houses."

"Ah. Do come in."

They stepped into the gloom.

"This way." The speaker turned and drifted into a side hall past barely visible artifacts and statuary that lined the hall. Some distance down this hall, the figure turned into a small room. He beckoned at the chairs and waited until they were seated.

"I am Parnar, who are you?"

"Jonathon."

"Dee."

"Ahhhhhhh, House Darthar." He nodded at them. "One hears word of the Head of House Darthar Na and here you are. Very pretty."

He sat and leaned back and carefully looked them over. "Sooooooo, problematic behavior and dying houses you said?"

"Yes," sighed Jonathon.

Dee looked past Parnar's head at the green eyes that blinked from the wall.

"And?" asked Parnar.

"Some houses have become no more, recently," stated Jonathon.

"Word did come to us of that." Parnar nodded.

"Problematic behavior," said Dee.

Parnar shrugged. "Matter of viewpoint, I believe." He made a small gesture. Black things stood on either side of him.

"Not required," said Jonathon.

"Matter of viewpoint." He looked at Jonathon and Dee. "Sooooooo, it is House Darthar, major and minor, that is creating the problem. Should have guessed as much." He nodded at them. "It would be most unfortunate for both houses to loose their heads, so to speak."

Parnar looked around. "Did I hear something?" And shook his head. "Of course not. Soooooo, what shall we do about you two?"

"Pour coffee," suggested Dee. "You have rather poor hospitality here in this house."

"Rethink," stated Jonathon. "There are too few of us as it is."

"Ah um, we can't keep you in a dungeon," said Parnar. "Although we do have a rather extensive one way down deep."

"Ah um," said Jonathon.

"You could join with us?" suggested Parnar.

"You the scumbags that killed my parents?" growled Dee. "I want to return the favor!"

"No! That was some other, ah um, scumbag, a more impulsive one." He sat up. "However, it does seem that you are about to join them, in a manner of speaking."

"Bad idea!" snapped Dee.

"Keep him alive, Dee."

Parnar stared at Jonathon.

She nodded. The Furleen launched themselves from the walls, shredding the black things. Two held Parnar in place, in his chair, while four flowed out the door. The rest sat in dark corners as Purr Cat slipped around Parnar and sat next to Dee. She yawned widely at Parnar, teeth glittering in the soft orange light of the room.

"I think," suggested Dee to Parnar, "that they would like to have you for dinner." She nodded. Four hounds thumped down and raced out the door.

Dee smiled at Parnar. "They won't hurt anyone, just herd them here."

Jonathon stood and stretched. "Word came that some stone house collapsed killing all within." He gently touched the mantlepiece and watched it crumble. "This is a very old structure as the people measure time." He stepped aside as a woman and three children ran into the room.

"Husband?" She gasped. "Why did you let those beasts into the house? They pushed us here! What happened to that mantlepiece?" She stomped over and glared down at him and pointed a quivering finger at a Furleen. "And one of those . . . things sharpened its claws on my new table."

Jonathon sat and watched and waited. "Lovely children," he said.

The woman said something and two pots and a number of cups appeared. She poured for them all and sat, telling her children to sit close to her and to sit up straight.

"Who are our guests?" she demanded.

"Jonathon."

"Dee."

Parnar nodded. "House Darthar and House Darthar Na."

"Oh," gasped the woman. "You poor dear. Word came of your parent's death. A terrible thing."

"Yes," said Dee, sipping from her cup.

Jonathon looked at Parnar. "Sooooo?"

Parnar slumped and nodded, throwing both of his arms around his youngest daughter who had just crawled into his lap.

"Over and done with?" asked Jonathon.

Parnar nodded.

"True promise," said Jonathon. "No speak on this? Over and done?"

"True promise," rasped Parnar.

"Dear?" His wife stared at him.

He waggled one hand. "Small piece of business." Then he stared around the room. All the beasts were gone.

"Sorry about your table," said Dee.

Jonathon stood. "Will you be safe?"

Parnar nodded. "We will be that."

Dee smiled at the woman. "Good coffee. Thank you."

"Most welcome," she said. She peered under the table. There was nothing there.

Two days later, as they ate a middle of the day meal, Dee and her daughters, Jonathon walked into the room frowning darkly.

Dee poured and shoved a cup across the table at him. "Sit, please."

He did. And picked up the cup and took a sip.

"What?"

"Some house attacked Darthar suta Farbin. Did small damage. A young male, a young impulsive male, died."

"Oh, Jonathon." She refilled his cup. "Will the other sub-houses out there be all right rather than being here?"

"Oh yes. Rinil, fourth brother, and Aberly, third sister, are seeing to that."

"Why didn't that group come here?"

"Ah um. They are very reclusive. Always have been. But they are very clever craftsmen, very clever. If that male had remained inside he would have been safe." He sipped and looked at her. "You mustn't be impulsive."

"Do you, or they, have any idea who did that?"

He nodded. "We are going to visit those ones."

"We?"

"Me, Aranda, and Hofga. You may come if you wish."

She nodded. "Yes. I think that I would like to do that."

"Tomorrow." He stood. "Some small planning to do. See you at breakfast." And left the room.

Dee looked at her daughters. "So, tell me how your lessons are doing."

"Oh, mother!" said Tiela.

Winala began to explain.

After breakfast as the small group walked toward the outside door, she said, "Wait here." And tugged Jonathon down the hall and stopped.

"What?"

"Tell me, Jonathon, about your skills."

"What?"

"I saw you touch that mantlepiece and I saw what happened. So tell me."

He nodded. "You know that each house has, umm ah, special, ah, skills?"

Yes."

He watched her very carefully. "My house, the main house, has special skills that are, um, of a protective nature. We are the ones, aided by your parents, that wrapped your house in its many layered wards, so deep that nothing Feyra can affect it." He blinked.

"And?" she pushed. "What else?"

He took one of her hands in his. "A reflection of protective defense is a destructive offense." He stared into her eyes. "You saw a bit of that in your bedroom when we first met."

"Oh, yes. That."

He nodded. "House Darthar, all parts, have always been careful, so very careful, and guarded, so very well guarded, that few have ever known, or seen, umm, our skills. That includes your's, House Darthar Na."

She nodded back. "Thank you. I was beginning to suspect something like that. But some are seeing those skills now."

He smiled at her, a soft, gentle smile. "Yes. Unfortunately. I keep forgetting how new you are, how new you really are to all of this."

She laughed. "An understatement if there ever was one. Shall we go?"

"Yes."

Jonathon, Aranda, Hofga, and Dee stood near the great stone and wood structure.

"Pretty impressive building," observed Dee. "In a dark sort of a way."

Jonathon nodded, and indicated the building with his chin. "This is House Farthan. Remember Arza?"

Dee nodded back. "Yes, I do. Pompous, self important."

Hofga huffed laughter.

"They are the ones that attacked suta Farbin. This structure is heavily warded."

"Maybe not good enough," boomed Hofga. He stomped one foot. The ground rolled in a deep wave toward and under the structure. It swayed and creaked and resettled.

"Humbah, maybe it is good enough," observed

Aranda, banging Hofga on one shoulder.

"Prata!" suggested Hofga.

Dee looked puzzled at him.

"A not nice word," explained Aranda. He grinned. "But that is our Hofga."

Hofga grumbled something under his breath at him.

"So," said Jonathon. "We take the wards away first." He looked at Dee. "Call the hounds, please? All of them."

Dee smiled and did.

Sixteen hounds milled around them. One bumped Dee with his forehead. "Good boy, Moe." She rubbed the top of his nose. "We need a large ring around us."

Moe gurgled softly at the others and soon the four stood in a large open space encircled by Inferno Hounds, all staring at Dee, waiting for her to tell them what to do next.

Aranda looked at them and then from Dee to Jonathon. "Now that is truly frightening."

A few of the hounds snorted steam.

Hofga laughed. "I like it, them!"

Jonathon pulled a small scroll from a side pocket. "Now we get rid of the wards.." He looked at Dee. "Remember this? Your distant cousin gave it to us." She nodded and remembered when Pardosh had given them the scroll.

He read the scroll and said, "Done." He stepped

up and kicked the door into the interior of the building.

"Dee, you remember their real name?"

"Yes."

"Call them all outside, please."

Arza stood there and glared at them, with two women, two sons, and three daughters.

"How dare you! Jonathon!"

Dee punched him in the nose.

Jonathon and Aranda stopped anyone from moving. Hofga laughed, and grinned at Dee. "Never saw that before. Very nice!"

"Arza," said Jonathon.

"What!" He mopped at this nose with a large handkerchief turning red. "Why are you here? With her! Most ill mannered!"

"House Farbin was attacked. By you and your's. A young male died. There is a price for that." Jonathon slowly looked over the sons and the daughters.

"Nooooooo," wailed the older of the two women.

Dee blanched.

Arza wobbled and stared and gasped, "Take me. But not one of them. I beg you. Not one of them." He dropped to his knees.

Jonathon looked down at him. "Not so pompous now." He kicked him. "Stand up!"

Arza scrambled to his feet and struggled to re-establish his dignity.

His first wife kicked him in the ankle. "If one of

our offspring dies, I will kill you if Jonathon does not!"

The second wife nodded.

Jonathon stepped close to Arza. "If the Head answers one small question true, no one dies."

"Ask," rasped Arza. "Ouch!" One of the hounds had puffed steam at him.

Dee frowned at that hound. Hofga grinned.

Jonathon suppressed his smile. The children stared wide-eyed at the immense beasts.

"Ask!"

"Who is responsible for that dark thing so many got involved with. Few have died, um, so far."

Arza sagged and looked from wife to wife. "Will they be safe? And my children?"

Jonathon nodded. "There is a small safe place for all to live very, very safely."

Arza nodded. "I will tell only you." He leaned forward and whispered in Jonathon's ear. And stepped back.

"True?" asked Jonathon.

Arza nodded.

"True promise that it is so?"

"True promise," rasped Arza.

"True promise that you and your's will not speak of this?"

"True promise."

Jonathon held a small ball in one hand. "None die but payment is due." He tossed the sphere through the shattered door. A gift from the Farbin.

Inside the building something flashed blue and faded away.

The structure began to bow inward and sag as it melted and flowed in upon itself. Soon there was only a great wet and boggy spot.

The second wife kicked Arza in this other ankle. "Now where do we live, Prata?"

Hofga grinned at her.

Jonathon told Arza and sent the family there.

"The Farbin?" Dee looked at him.

Jonathon nodded. "House Farthan will learn humility and maybe a few other things." He pointed at the great swamp forming. "Eventually they will be released and be allowed to build a new house. They will have to find a different spot though."

Dee nodded. The hounds were gone. "Let's go home. Also."

Chapter Fifteen

Truly Not Nice.

House Darthar Na.

They were finishing an end of the day meal, Jonathon and Dee. She had spent a great part of it beginning entertained by her daughters and taking a lesson from Ar.

Relatives were forming small conversation groups and breaking apart and reforming. Jonathon had told them everything. Well, almost everything.

Now they were by themselves were Jonathon and Dee, sitting quiet, looking out the large window at the forest, sipping coffee.

"This is going to take careful planning."

"Sure," agreed Dee.

"We cannot lose the Head of House Darthar Na."

She laughed. "Well, I certainly can agree with that."

"Stay home."

"NO! I want that guy. I have some very personal reasons for that." She glared at him. "I am not staying home."

He nodded. "Very careful planning."

She nodded. And refilled his cup. And smiled.

"What?"

"Oh, not much. Just thinking of something that Ar and I were discussing."

"Umm?"

"He was just exploring a new skill for me, that's all."

"Ah."

Two days later Jonathon banged on the door to the Training Hall. It was locked. "Dee, you in there?"

The door unlocked and swung open. He stepped in and stopped.

She was dripping sweat. Ar was in a corner, in a deep protective crouch.

She smiled, then laughed at Jonathon's expression. "Just practicing. This one is hard work. I need at least two days more. All right?"

Jonathon watched Ar unbend and then nodded at her. "Yes. Two more days." He pointed at the door. "Locked?"

"Yep. Didn't want anyone to walk in during practice and, ah, getting injured. Just a safety precaution." She headed for the door. "Worked up quite an appetite. Let's go eat." And laughed. "Lots."

As they headed down the hall, she called her daughters to join them.

Two beaming girls greeted the pair as they

stepped into the room. They were feeding tibits to their Ice Cats.

Dee sighed. "Oh, well, that's what happens, I suppose." She sat and dumped large quantities of the food onto her plate and lessor amounts on Jonathon's. The girls served themselves having decided that certain items on the menu were no longer edible even though they were a few days before.

"Mother," said Winala, who was turning into the more studious one, "we need some time with Ar also."

Dee pushed the Ice Cat aside and hugged her. "It will be for just two more days then you may study as much as you wish. Eat!"

Jonathon was carefully studying Dee.

"What?"

"You have changed."

Both daughters stared at her.

Dee shrugged. "Probably lost some weight practicing. This one is really hard, hard work." She dumped another load onto her plate. Then refilled all the coffee cups. And began to eat. "Burned up lots of energy working on that skill."

He nodded. And sipped. "Good coffee."

"A gift. Guess who?"

"Hofga."

"Nope." She grinned. "It is from Arza."

"Ummmmm."

Dee laughed. "Thought that you would be surprised."

He took another sip. "May I ask?"

She shrugged. "I have no idea why he did that. Maybe he feels guilty or something."

"About your practice."

"Nope. It is a surprise, another surprise." She refilled his cup, her eyes twinkling.

He began to worry, a little.

For two days, Dee practiced inside the locked Training Hall, and ate huge meals, and slept long hours.

On the third morning, she stepped in, ready for breakfast, and hugged a very surprised Ar.

"Thanks," she said. "I know you didn't want to do that, and probably still think that it is a bad idea, but it works and I really have control." She kissed his forehead, and sat. And heaped her plate full. "I have very good control."

Finally, she sat back, and sipped from her cup and smiled around the table. "Well, daughters, guess who gets to go back to their lessons?"

Tiela frowned, a little.

Winala grinned.

Dee looked at Jonathon. "So, let's plan." She laughed. "You already have, haven't you?"

"Yes."

Shooing her daughters from the room she called Hofga, Aranda, and Frandel.

Jonathon began to explain, stressing that Dee was to be very, very careful. He pointed out that their success depended on that house coming outside to attack them in the open fields around their dwelling.

When he finished, he frowned darkly at her with down turned corners of his mouth. "You cannot get involved."

She nodded. "No problemo, dude." And laughed. "I will stay well clear of all the turmoil on the ground. But!"

"What?"

"I want the one responsible for my parents and all that happened."

He nodded.

"Promise me, Jonathon, promise me."

He nodded again and held out his cup. She refilled it, watching his eyes. "Dee, he will be the only one out there with pure white hair. He is your's. True promise."

Tears sparkled in her eyes as she leaned sideways and kissed him. "Thank you, Jonathon." She leaned back and grinned. "And don't worry, please?"

Hofga looked at her from the corners of his eyes. He could tell even if the others couldn't. She was holding something back. He could feel it. It was very not nice.

Dee stood. "Going upstairs for awhile. See you later, group." And laughed. "You too, Hofga."

They all stared at her as she left the room. Then three friends stared at him.

Jonathon looked around the table. "No idea."

Then he spread a very detailed map out on the table and began to discuss with them how he thought that they ought to proceed.

Finally they were done.

"It will be interesting," said Aranda.

"We will do hard as possible," said Jonathon.

Frandel nodded. "Very messy."

Hofga grinned at them. "Good!" he boomed.

They relocated to another room, ate a meal, and rested.

Everyone did that, rest, for a number of days.

A Great Battle Ground.

They stood just inside the dense forest and peered out. The house across the open meadow was a true castle of dark, moss overgrown stone with a high outer wall, battlements and towers. Rearing high in the central space was the main building, tall towers on each corner, all dark rough cut timber upper stories set on heavy lower walls of dark stone.

"Pretty impressive." Dee stared at it.

Jonathon nodded. "House Narkalar. Usually allied with House Hamptus, their main supporter. Hamptus will do nothing here. Their way is to gain value not loss. We will speak to them later. With House Narkalar no longer leading, the rest will withdraw. That idea will die!"

He looked at Dee.

She winked. "I know. I will stay clear of the

turmoil on the ground." She nodded.

All around them, in the darkness of the dense forest, they could hear movement.

"They are all here," explained Dee. "All the house beasts are arriving. It will take a few moments for the hounds to get ready."

The men looked around. And then they saw them, slowly beginning to glow. The hounds were raising their internal temperatures.

Heavy footfalls announced the arrival of the ten Kartar, the great grizzly bear shaped beasts with the heavy green scales. They pushed to the edge of the forest and peered out.

Soft purring rumbled around them as the Furleen oozed into position.

"Tell me when, Jonathon." Dee edged close to the opening in front of them.

"Now, Dee, now."

"I will watch careful," she said, stepping out. She soared up and up and up, floating in wide circles on long, white, feather covered, wings. She joined the eight great eagle-like Tarken as they drifted in lazy circles, waiting for her.

The men stared and watched until they saw her enter the flock, one set of white wings among all the dark brown ones, all cutting lazy patterns in the sky high over their heads.

Hofga laughed. "Clear of the turmoil on the ground, Jonathon, clear of the turmoil. Might as well begin. Those hounds are rather obvious.

The Inferno Hounds were now bright red, puffing black smoke from their mouths.

"Yes." Jonathon stepped out and walked to the mid-point between the castle and the forest behind them. He waited.

Aranda stood to his left, Frandel to his right. Hofga walked past Jonathon, nodded, and stomped his right foot.

The ground heaved, the great shock wave rolled in a long swell toward the outer wall. And washed past it, into the interior space.

All heard the loud crack of breaking stone.

Hofga stomped and stomped, faster and faster and faster. Dust billowed into the sky from one spot along that outer wall. Rock tumbled from the growing dust cloud and bounced across the grass.

Angry shouts could be heard coming from the house.

Hofga stepped back and laughed. "Guess we got their attention." He stepped further back.

As the gentle breeze blew away the dust they could see a large rubble strewn gap in the outer wall and the depression where the ground had sunk some small amount.

Dee peered down from the center of the circling Tarken. Black things were pouring from the main structure, lurching toward the gap in the wall. Dee told the hounds.

Sixteen glowing objects trailing fire bounded from the forest toward the opening. They scorched black paths across the green of the meadow. Small fires broke out in the forest.

She could see the Furleen flowing in a dense pack to one side and pouring fluid soft up and over the wall into the interior space and blurring into the grass.

The eight giant Kartar trudged after the hounds.

From high above, she could hear in the sudden silence the four men taunting the House members inside the central structure. She swooped lower and stared. Jonathon was shimmering. Aranda and Frandel ran further to the sides.

She soared high above her flock and peered down at the activity on the ground. From far below she could hear the booming laughter of Hofga and the loud crash as a corner of the main building collapsed.

In the gap of the outer wall, fire was blasting in a wide arc as black things sizzled and died.

The Furleen poured into the main building through the great hole in the collapsed corner and disappeared.

The hounds, following shouted orders from Frandel, parted and allowed the Tarkar to trundle thorough. They thumped into the center of the castle wall, crashed through the windows and into the interior.

The hounds were now attacking the damaged corner, ripping and tearing more and more pieces away, threatening to undermine the tower at that corner.

The door to the castle flew open and they poured out, wreathed in black, hurtling toward Jonathon, who stood and waited.

"I WILL KILL YOU ALL," screamed the lead figure. "PAINFULLY! YOU WILL NOT STOP OUR GREAT AND NOBLE CAUSE!"

Furleen flowed in a wave from that same door and poured over the figures at the back, eliminating them.

Jonathon crossed his arms and laughed. Hofga, standing nearby, laughed even louder. And danced up and down.

As the crowd ran past the damaged place in the outer wall, Frandel gestured. A green wave ripped away those on the side close to where he stood.

Aranda cast and tangled the survivors on the other side who crashed and thrashed on the ground.

Jonathon jumped back as Hofga ran toward the dense forest, toward one of the not burning patches.

Hounds and Kartar scattered as the tower and great section of the front wall puffed dust from multiple seams and began to crumble outward taking a large piece of the roof with it.

The remainder of those inside ran screaming from the house, leaping from the door and a number of windows.

The screeching Head swung a great black thing at Jonathon who stepped back, then in, brushed the weapon aside and knocked him sprawling, his ornate hat spinning away.

Dee could see the white hair as the figure sprang to his feet.

"MINE!" she howled as she plunged downward in a steep wing tucked in near freefall and landed nearby with a great thump.

Jonathon, Aranda, and Frandel took one look and ran as hard as they could back. Everyone scattered in every direction, away, away, away.

She towered above him, leaned over and clamped one hand around his neck and lifted him up and up, close to her face, close to long, gleaming canines. She hissed, a soft grumbling snarl. "I have you, tasty small man. You forced my parents to flee." The long tongue lazily rasped over his cheek.

She stomped some surviving black thing trying to attack her deep into the meadow.

"You killed my parents." The long tongue rasped over his cheek again, ripping the skin. She sniffed at him and growled. "Fresh blood."

"You denied me my identity." She pinched his side with two talons on her free hand. And watched the stain spread on his clothes.

Great red eyes peered into his staring ones. She hissed, "How slow can you die? It seems to be something you like to deliver to others. Shall we see how long it can take?"

She kicked one male, daring to attack her with a

weapon, up and over the standing wall to thump heavily and tumble into a loose-limbed heap..

Then she leaped and landed next to the partially destroyed castle and clambered up the side to stand on a piece of the still intact roof.

"So little man," she gurgled. "What shall we do with you?" She jabbed him with a talon and waited for the screaming to stop.

"How about I break both of your legs, leave you up here to watch while I eat your family?"

A large shape landed on the high tower nearby, and folded great grey wings.

"Dee, don't." It peered down at the Karthan, the fierce female predator from their earliest primitive times. "Don't."

The beast reared up and up on its rear legs and stared at the grey thing. "Jonathon? Is that you?"

"Yes." One long arm gestured. "There were three high house whose members had gathered here. One house fled, one house died, and this family is badly damaged. At least two-thirds are dead. And this structure will collapse soon."

The great red eyes flickered fire as she looked at him. "Is that enough for all that this one has done." She shook the moaning House Head back and forth.

"Yes." He floated upward. "Jump down. Become Dee again. You are scaring everyone, even the house beasts."

She leaned and peered down, Nothing was

moving down there. Everything was hiding in the dense part of the forest not already burning.

She leaped, landed with a dull thump, turned and hurtled the family Head through a high window into the building and bounded over the outer wall and ran to the forest edge. And collapsed.

So did the castle.

Her eyes popped open.

She looked around. She was lying in a large bed in a very large bedroom.

In a chair nearby, Jonathon slept sitting up.

Ar slipped into the room. "There is lots of food in the adjoining room, Princess. And some business to attend to after you eat."

Dee threw the covers back, picked up the robe draped across the end of the bed and slipped it on.

Then she shook his shoulder. "Come on, Jonathon. Let's get something to eat."

His eyes flew open.

"Come on, I am hungry," she grumbled, shaking his shoulder again.

"What?"

She headed through the adjoining door and smiled at her daughters who leaped up and hugged her from both sides.

"You slept a long time," whispered Winala.

Tiela wiped her eyes with her sleeve. "Two whole days."

Dee gently pushed them away and sat. "Tiela, please serve the food while Winala pours the coffee." She laughed. "And don't mind Jonathon, I don't think that he slept very well."

When all had been served, Dee began to eat. "Certainly worked up an appetite." She held out her cup. "Please?"

Karanly bounded in and dropped into a chair. "Eyes are a little baggy, Dee. What has my brother been up to?" She munched on a piece of toast and glowered at him.

Winala filled his cup. Again.

His eyes jumped from face to face and stopped on Dee's. "Frightened everything." And started on his second helping.

Finally feeling pleasantly stuffed, Dee finished her coffee and went next door to get dressed.

She sat on the throne, Ar standing by her right side, and looked down and out at the folk gathered in this room.

Jonathon, Aranda, Frendel, and Hofga stood toward her right side, not too close, not too far away.

On her left there was a cluster of individuals who were, more or less, cringing. Purr Cat and Moe sat behind them, not too close, not too far away.

Ar leaned close and whispered in her ear. She nodded. And beckoned Jonathon to step close.

"Great Lord, who are those ones?" She pointed.

He bowed very formally, very deeply, and said, "Those, Princess, are the survivors of House Narkalar." He indicated the small male standing by himself, nervously shifting from foot to foot, his eyes jumping from her to Jonathon. He was carefully ignoring the others. "That one is the Head of House Hamptus, the ones who fled."

She nodded, and smiled a smile of no humor at them all. "What do you propose for them?"

Jonathon pointed at a young woman standing behind the others casting fearful glances at the two house beasts, and crooked his finger. "Step close, Eltrill."

She carefully edged around the others, walked cautious steps over to him, stopped, and bowed, first to Jonathon, then to Dee, and straightened up.

Jonathon beckoned again. Karanly strode up to his side and bowed to Dee.

"I do propose, Princess, with your permission, that Eltrill remain here in your house and learn from Karanly, first sister, all she must know to function as Head of House Narkalar." Family members gasped. She was a young level daughter. "When Karanly is satisfied, and only then, House Narkalar may rebuilt their dwelling. The rest will also dwell here and there, learning from each of our kin until such time as Head Eltrill decides that it is proper for them to rejoin her as family."

He bowed to Dee, then to Eltrill, and said, "If this

is acceptable, Princess Eltrill?"

She gasped, stepped forward and dropped to her knees and bowed to Dee. "Yes, most so, if this Princess does so agree?"

"Stand," said Dee.

As Eltrill straightened up, Dee smiled at her. "Most welcome, Princess Eltrill." Then Dee indicated the others. "I do think that living with House Darthar suta Milaton would be a good place to begin, um, if the Great Lord does agree?"

Jonathon nodded. "It will happen."

She whispered to Ar who fetched a chair and set it on the left side of the throne. Dee indicated the chair and smiled at Eltrill. "Do join us, Princess."

Eltrill hurried up, sat and watched the remains of her family walk from the hall. No one looked back.

Dee pointed. "You! Come here!"

He gasped and hurried to the base of the platform.

"Your true name! Tell me!"

He cleared his throat. "Zananan a'Destar a'Naden a'Gorten a'Narkalar d'Hamptus, Princess."

Dee looked at Jonathon. "And what shall we do with him, Lord?"

Him struggled with ever weakening knees.

"That one owes many houses much for all the damage that he was party to. We shall see that his house pays appropriately." He nodded at Eltrill. "Especially to House Narkalar, is that not so, Princess."

"Yes," said Eltrill. "Such poor council, such dark council, such weak council bears a heavy burden." She bowed her head to Jonathon. "Perhaps, Great Lord, after he has satisfied all the others, we may speak upon what would be, ummm, fair and just with us?"

Jonathon nodded. "Yes. Just so." He looked at the small man. "You may leave us. We will call you as necessary." And watched him hurry from the room.

Then he waved his three friends forward and nodded at Dee."They have been told to think long and careful as to what, ummmm ah, reward would please them." He smiled a soft, gentle smile at them. "Within reason, of course."

Hofga laughed. It echoed off the walls. He winked at Dee, waved to Jonathon, and left.

Aranda and Frendel thanked them both very formally and left.

Dee stood. "I am still quite hungry. Do join us, Eltrill." She strolled from the hall, her arm linked through one of Karanly's, and whispered to her, "I think that I am catching on to all of this."

It was three days later and all were well rested.

Dee and Jonathon were idly strolling about in the large meadow in front of her house, enjoying the warm sun and the quiet.

More or less quiet.

Tiela and Winala were flying in great circles, white wings shining in the sun, playing with the Ice

Cats. Or perhaps the Ice Cats were playing with them.

The game appeared to be one of Ice Cat stalking and catching the girls with the Ice Cats leaping high in the air and touching, or trying to touch, one daughter or the other with soft paws.

The girls were laughing and the Ice Cats were making long arching leaps purring loudly.

Dee pointed up at the large flock making slow circles high above. "Everything is going home."

Jonathon looked up.

Three pair of the Tarken floated off in three different directions.

The hounds charged from the house into the meadow and broke into smaller groups and hurtled into the forest. The remaining four trotted over and sat near Dee and Jonathon and watched the game being played across the meadow from them.

The Furleen pride joined them, chirped soft call to Dee, and flowed fluid soft into the forest.

Purr Cat stretched out and basked in the warmth.

The Kartar clumped from the house and thumped off in various directions, leaving one pair to stand and watch everything.

Jonathon nodded at her. "The families are leaving as well. Your house is going to be very quiet once again." Eltrill walked from the house, talking softly with Karanly as they crossed the meadow.

Eltrill smiled as a small Ice Cat galloped from the house and up to her side. She smiled at Jonathon. "She is a gift from sub-house Milaton." Tears wandered down her cheeks. "I have no way to apologize for my House or anything else that happened. My father had gone strange some time ago but no-one in the family truly understood how strange. He really . . . ahhhhh, he almost killed us all."

Karanly hugged her and patted her back. "We know, Princess," she murmured, "we really do. And understand."

Jonathon nodded and beckoned Dee to walk with him to a far edge of the meadow. Then he spoke in a very soft voice so only she could hear. "Dee, I do not think that skill you learned should be taught to anyone else. That part of our distant long ago past is much too dangerous, much too dangerous,"

She nodded. "I agree. Let's go inside, have a snack, and drink a little coffee."

They walked that way, waving at the rest to remain and do whatever it was they felt like doing.

Chapter Sixteen

Not Another Thing?

House Darthar Na.

Time had passed very pleasantly.

Dee had studied with Ar as did her daughters.

Karanly had tutored Eltrill.

All in all, it was a very relaxing time.

Dee was learning more and more of her own background and the girls were learning more and more of their family history and various cultural behaviors.

Then one day, Dee sat up, stopped idly staring out the large window as she sipped from her cup, and realized how much time had really passed.

Tiela and Winala had reached the end of their growth spurt and looked to Dee to be like senior high school students as she remembered them from her people memories.

Then she decided that it was time for her to know her own family lineage in some detail.

She left the room and strolled down the hall, walked into a small, comfortable room, poured two cups full, and sat. And called.

Jonathon walked in and took the other cup, sat, and sipped.

"Yes?"

"I would like to know my family lineage in just as much detail as you know your's. Can you find that something?"

He nodded. "We do have many family records. It will take a few days, but I can do that?"

"Thanks."

He nodded, finished his coffee, and left.

It was three days later.

They sat and sipped.

He nodded. "You are Daliera Fontala, which is quite unusual as we rarely use two names."

"Why?"

"Tradition, I think. The reason for that is lost in the very long ago and was never written down. Fontala may mean something but it would take much to find that."

"And?"

"Your true name is Daliera Fontala etc., etc., d'Darthar Na. All those etc. are the same as mine as we are, after all, one Darthar with two branches. You have cousin-houses a'Dalir a'Namata a'Induna a'Patal a'Angorson a'Anathor." He sipped. "Now you know them as well. You already know and met many of the sub-houses."

She nodded. "Jonathon?"

"Ummmmm?"

"Can we go visit them, all of them?"

"Ah ummmm. You already met Pardosh d'Angorson and Kraz d'Anathor." He nodded. "We could visit the others. I will have to take some time to find the locations of those, umm ah, cousin-houses."

"I would like that."

He stood. "Another day or so." And was gone.

Dee was in the training hall talking to her daughters about their flying. The skill not only produced wings but massive changes in the body to support those immense additions. The end result was that afterwards one needed to eat and to drink very large amounts. She thought that children, being children, were not paying enough attention to that aspect, eating and drinking lots.

"So," said Dee, throwing an arm around the shoulders of daughters, who were looking askance at her and the need to eat and drink lots instead of doing something more interesting. She looked at Ar. "I can block their usage of that skill, if I wish?"

Ar, realizing full well what the problem was, bowed deeply, and replied, all serious tone of voice, "Yes, you may do that, Princess."

Dee sent Tiela and Winala off to eat and to drink and to rest. The pair straggled from the hall looking very daughter unhappy and feeling that they been very poorly treated.

Dee smiled at Ar. "Thank you."

He nodded. "They will understand soon."

Jonathon strolled into the hall. "What did you do to them?"

"Small lesson. Not much."

"Ummmmm, Shall we go?"

"Let's. Who first?"

"Dalir."

Ar headed from the hall and down the hall to see that a certain meal had plenty of nourishing parts to it.

Dee slowly turned and stared at the smoky air and great burned over spot.

On all sides of the structure grey ash and smoldering remains stretched a long way into the surrounding forest.

"Forest fire?"

"Ummmm, no." Jonathon pointed. "This was centered over the house. It is a very wide circle with a very sharp edge." Then he indicated the roof of the building. "Lots of scorch marks, but no real damage."

He stepped up and knocked on the door.

"Speak," said someone.

"Jonathon and your cousin Dee come to visit."

The door swung in.

She leaned out. "Dee? I have no cousin by that name. Begone!"

Dee stepped up and jammed her foot in the doorway, preventing the door from closing completely.

"I am Daliera Fontala, Head of House Darthar Na."

The door was jerked wide.

"Daliera?"

"Yes. May we enter?"

"OH! Do come in."

Dee and Jonathon stepped inside.

The woman turned to him after firmly closing the door. "I am Parlente, Head of House Dalir." She smiled. "You are a shock and a surprise, cousin. All word was much confused and very hard to believe."

She spun and beckoned them to come along, down the short hall, and into a rather pleasant room furnished with very comfortable chairs set around a low table.

Parlente filled their cups before her own and waited for them to sit. She looked at Dee. "Word came of wild destruction of a great house and very strange happenings. It sounded fanciful and unreal. All wonder about House Darthar Na. Your parent's did tell not why they fled."

Dee looked at Jonathon who told a very carefully edited story. Palente filled their cups.

"It is good," said Palente, "to have a Head in House Darthar Na. And offspring."

Dee smiled and asked how House Dalir was faring and why they had such a great burned area all around the house.

Parlente slumped in her chair and sipped. "A male pounded on our door not much long ago and shouted angry demand at us. That one demanded that we gift over the youngest daughter, our fourth daughter. We refused such. And that happened?"

Jonathon sat straighter. "Who?"

"Unknown. He did not properly introduce, just made crude suggestion."

"Ummmmmm."

Dee looked from him to her. "What did this guy, ah, not nice male look like?"

"Didn't see much," replied Parlente. "Short. Very angry. As soon as that one shouted ugly, I slammed the door."

Parlente beckoned in a male and her four daughters and introduced them to Dee and Jonathon.

The man bowed and then frowned at four daughters who were staring at Dee. They gasped and hastily bowed.

Then all went into a larger room and shared a meal and talked about this and that.

Parlente walked with them to the door. "A true pleasure to visit with our cousin, Daliera."

Stepping outside, Dee took another look at the burned over area. "Jonathon, is that normal for someone to demand another's daughter like that?"

"No, it is not. Not normal at all. Very strange."

"O.K." She nodded. "Shall we go?"

He nodded.

And they did. Go.

The grass plain spread in all directions in soft waves. The air ruffled along over the grass in a gentle breeze. The grass was tall, up to their waists.

He turned her around. "House Namata."

"It looks like they don't take very good care of it."

The building had high walls with finger thin spires stretching toward the sky. Three of them had been bent and leaned at odd angles to each other.

She walked up to the door and gently knocked.

"Who beats upon my door?" snarled someone.

"No one is beating upon your door." She knocked gently again.

"A strange name to have, No One. Go away!"

Jonathon stepped up and thumped on the door. "Jonathon and Dee come to visit."

"Jonathon and what?"

Jonathon thumped again. "Dee!"

"Why does your companion keep changing their label, Jonathon?" The door slowly opened.

He peered out. "Ah. It is truly you," he said to Jonathon. "Do come in.' He opened the door wide. "And bring whatever it is called with you."

Dee grumbled at Jonathon as they stepped inside, "Are all my relatives this peculiar?"

"Ummm."

Dee looked at the man who was taller and wider than either herself or Jonathon. "I am Daliera Fontala. What do you call yourself?" She glared at him.

He bent and stared at her. "Truly? Daliera of the Fontala?"

She nodded.

He laughed. "Most welcome, Princess! Most welcome. Word said that you had died horribly in some strange people place." He bowed very formally. "I am most delighted to see you. I am Fam, Head of House Hamata. Come, let us sit and talk." He spun and led them deep into the building and then into a hall and finally into room with a table set against one wall.

He sat and poured three cups of coffee and smiled at her. "An only child. Have you and Jonathon mated?"

"No," said Jonathon.

"Ah well." Fam sipped. "How is your house, Daliera?"

"Fine."

"Most good. Have you had any strange visitors?"

"No."

"Most good."

"Have you?" asked Jonathon.

Fam nodded. "Not very much past. Most peculiar."

"Ummmm."

"I have three sons," stated Fam. "Only. A not nice individual banged on our door and made insult remarks."

"Like?" asked Dee.

"Demanded a present of one of our offspring. A

female. I told this not nice one that he was pas gar tak and uninformed. Then he shouted at us something unintelligible and broke three spines. Special workmen are coming to repair what requires repairing."

"Ummm ah," said Jonathon.

"Ummm?" asked Fam.

Jonathon told him.

"Did you see this, ah, individual?" asked Dee.

"Not a bit. Wouldn't open the door to something like that." He looked at Dee. "Care for a small bit of food, Princess Cousin? Always do that now." He pointed.

The table across the room was set.

"Thank you, we would." Dee stood and watched as three young men walked into the room, all tall and wide like their father.

"Renda, Anlada, and Uonit," said Fam. "This is Jonathon and Daliera Fontala, Princess Cousin of House Darthar Na."

Dee received three very warm smiles as they bowed to her and Jonathon.

Then all sat and had a snack. It was a number of light fluffy pastries.

"Really good." Dee licked the frosting from her lips.

"House speciality," said Renda.

Then, when it was polite to do so, Jonathon stood and thanked Fam for it all and said, " We have to be on our way."

Fam walked them to the door. "Do come again, House Darthar and House Darthar Na."

Dee bowed. "Thank you."

"Yes." Jonathon walked outside with her. The door thumped shut.

"What is going on?"

"Strange," he replied.

"I'd say so," agreed Dee. "Let's go."

The door was set flush in a towering rock face that was set well back from the highest tide line. The beach and the rock face stretched in both directions, out of sight, all bluish rock and grey sand.

Dee looked at the door and rock face. "Gonna be hard to do damage to that."

They walked up and he knocked. "This is House Induna."

The door slid straight back and then sideways.

A young woman stepped into the opening. She was wearing a glittering silver chainmail shirt and holding a glowing orange mace. She watched them carefully.

"Jonathon and Dee come to visit," said Jonathon.

She nodded to him, carefully looked over Dee, and beckoned them inside, and stepped to one side. "Do come in." After scanning the beach in both directions, she stepped back in, and told the door closed.

She led them down the tunnel, around a bend, and into an open space filled with soft light from many globes fastened to the polished smooth surface of the rock walls.

A table was set, a coffee pot steamed.

She poured and sat.

"I am first daughter Armilin, Anointed One, Head of House Induna. You are?"

"Jonathon, Head, House Darthar."

"Welcome, Lord."

"Daliera Fontala, Head of House Darthar Na."

"Cousin?"

"I am that."

"Most welcome, Princess." She stood. "Come, our mother must see you." Armilin hurried into a narrow hall. "This way."

Jonathon leaned close and murmured. "Her mother is dying. She must be the Head. Armilin is to be the successor. That is what anointed signifies."

Dee nodded.

In the large bedroom, Armilin introduced them to her mother, Zean, who beckoned Dee to come close.

Piercing black eyes searched Dee's face. "Yes," came the feather soft voice. "Yes, I see the mother in the daughter. Most welcome, Daliera of the Fontala, Princess of the well favored House of Darthar Na." One finger beckoned Dee even closer, she had to bend slightly. "I wish to ask a favor of this Princess, the last favor I shall ask at the end of a many long life."

Dee nodded.

"My daughter," she said all gentle sigh, "the

warrior, swift and terrible, Armilin, is the Anointed One. I would have her stay some at House Darthar Na to learn the soft and gentle firm ways of House Head, Daliera Princess. That is the favor that I ask."

Dee glanced at Jonathon who gave the faintest of nods.

"Of course," said Dee. She looked at Armilin. "If the Anointed One does agree."

Armilin bowed to her mother and then to Dee.

"Go now," whispered the figure in the bed.

"I go," stated Armilin, becking Dee and Jonathon from the room. "Second sister Eagta with stand for me, no conflict." With long strides she led them outside.

Jonathon nodded and spoke to Dee.

Karanly appeared. "My!" She smiled at Armilin, and took her arm.

Dee opened the door. "Do come in." She led her party down the hall and turned into a good room for visiting.

She passed filled cups to all and then explained to Karanly what the favor was.

Karanly grinned at Jonathon.

Eltrill walking in, looked at those already there, and took a seat. Dee handed her a filled cup, and made the introductions.

"Eltrill, Princess, Head of House Narkalar. Armilin, Princess, Anointed One, Head of House Induna. Karanly, first sister, House Darthar, teacher."

Eltrill stood and bowed to Armilin.

Armilin did the same to her.

Karanly smiled at her two students.

Dee looked at Armilin. "Is that the usual costume for Head?"

Armilin dropped into her chair. "Would you have me in attire other dress?"

Dee shook her head, and looked at Karanly, then Jonathon.

"The Head wears what the Head wears," stated Karanly. She nodded at Armilin.

Armilin sipped and looked at Eltrill as the Ice Cat slipped into the room and sat by her side. "House Narkalar. Word came of a great happening."

Eltrill nodded. "Most true." She scratched one fussy ear. "Here one learns much."

Karanly stood. "Come, Princess Armilin. I will show you to your quarters. They are next to those of Princess Eltrill."

The pair left.

Eltrill looked at Dee. "One rarely see warriors."

Jonathon sipped. "House Induna is noted for them, male and female."

Tiela and Winala hurtled into the room.

"Mother," asked Tiela, "who was that one?"

"The female in the silver glitter," added Winala.

"A guest," explained Dee. "She will be learning House Head with Eltrill from Karanly. So, she doesn't need to be bothered with questions from curious daughters."

"Yes, mother," they said in unison.

Early in the next day, Tiela and Winala were studying something new that Ar had just introduced to them when the Training Hall door opened and Armilin walked in.

She strode to the far end and began to practice. She flowed smoothly through the complicated patterns, spinning, leaping, attacking, retreating, the glowing orange mace formed long streaks of light in the air around her.

Tiela stood, fascinated by what she saw. That Princess was weaving around herself a shell of flashing orange. She nodded to Ar and walked over to take a closer watch. It definitely took a much closer inspection. She thought that it was beautiful.

She waited at a safe distance until, finally, Armilin stopped, face glowing exercise healthy, sweat soaked.

"It was beautiful," said Tiela.

Armilin nodded.

Tiela smiled. "Come this way. It is closer than going all the way up to your quarters."

Armilin nodded and followed her the short distance to a small room where the table was set for two. Tiela pointed at another door. "In there. Large wash facilities."

She sat as Armilin walked into the adjacent

room. Tiela poured her cup full, sipped, and heard the blasts of water start.

When Armilin walked out, smiling happily, Tiela poured her cup full.

Armilin sat, sipped, and nodded. "Very different, water shooting at one. Most pleasant."

"Mother's idea."

"Most clever."

"I would like to learn."

"Ummmmm."

"What you were just doing, those things that you did, in the Training Hall."

Armilin set her cup down and stared at Tiela with hard warrior eyes.

"I am first daughter," stated Tiela, "by a very small instance from my sister." She held her hand out, thumb and forefingers just touching slightly. "As small as can be. We are near twins."

Armilin stared. "Your mother had two?"

Tiela nodded.

"Word did not say so."

Tiela shrugged. "We, this House, are very private. We do prefer this, we do."

"Hard," stated Armilin. "Very hard. To learn."

Tiela sat up. "I would learn if you would teach."

Armilin nodded. "Every day, every day, exactly as I say. No discussion, just do!"

"Just so." Tiela stood. "I will tell Mother."

The sun was just high enough to shine into the room where Dee sat, eating breakfast, enjoying the quiet part of the day. Someone knocked.

"Enter."

Armilin did and sat as Dee poured and pushed a cup in her direction.

'Princess, I did not tell."

Dee smiled. "Tiela did. Work her hard. It will be good for her."

Armilin nodded. "Something other."

"Oh?"

Armilin told Dee of their strange visitor who banged on their door and made not nice demands.

"Third sister, Kitea, wished to chop that one's head from his shoulders for such saying, screaming she would do that thing. He hurried away."

"You didn't see that one?"

"No. The door was not opened for that one."

Dee nodded. "That one seems to be irritating many."

"A not safe behavior," stated Armilin, her finger tapping the orange glowing mace sitting next to her cup.

Dee refilled their cups, and nodded. "Yes. We shall have to learn who that irritating one is."

Armilin smiled. And began to eat.

After resting for two days, they journeyed out again.

Pardosh invited them in and nodded at them as they walked in. "Most welcome, Princess Cousin."

She smiled at him and followed him into a small room where it was set for three.

Dee sipped and looked from Pardosh to Jonathon. Jonathon nodded. "Any strange visitors come this way?"

Pardosh jumped to his feet. "Bent ugly that one! Screaming not nice, throwing things." He looked at Jonathon. "That one limped away." He dropped back into his chair. "Demanding!"

Dee grabbed the pot and refilled her cousin's cup.

"What?" asked Jonathon.

"That one demanded my youngest daughter. To be given. Horrible manners!" He sipped. "My first son rushed out and beat him before I could prevent it."

Dee cleared her throat.

"Yes?" asked Pardosh.

"What did he look like? Did he give a name?"

"No name! Impolite! Short, dressed all in black."

"Not him again." Dee sighed and looked at Jonathon.

He looked at Pardosh. "That one is the third son of the House Parthandar." Jonathon stood, walked over and bent close to Pardosh's ear.

"WHAT!" Something growled loudly.

Dee's eyes jerked in that direction. "What was that?"

"House demon," said her cousin. He grumbled at Jonathon, "Why is that one still among us?"

"Ummmmm. Mistake." Jonathon walked back and dropped into his chair, and emptied his cup, and stood.

Dee stood, thanked Pardosh, and headed outside.

Kraz opened the door and peered around one edge. "Gone?"

"Little short guy with a big mouth?" asked Dee.

Kraz looked at her and frowned. "I didn't notice a facial deformity. Terrible manners. Thought that the house had a daughter that he should have. He left. In a hurry. I tossed a krekit at him."

He led the pair into a side room, set with cups and a numbers of prepared dishes. He served after calling his son in.

"This is Ankar." Kraz smiled at Jonathon. "Tell Karanly to visit. They should meet."

Jonathon nodded and looked at Dee.

Karanly stepped into the room and smiled at Kraz and Ankar. "Lovely." She stepped around and hugged the young man. Then she kissed Kraz on the forehead. "All appear most well."

Kraz nodded. Ankar bowed to her. Karanly laughed, and sat, and began to eat. "Very good, also."

Kraz looked at Karanly. "Our son studies hard. Even if he doesn't want to."

Karanly winked at Ankar. "Maybe he ought to have a little time to visit House Darthar Na?" She looked at Dee.

Dee looked at Kraz. "May he do that?"

Kraz looked elsewhere. Ankar's eyes jumped from face to face.

"One people time week," stated Kraz firmly.

"Then," said Dee, "Ankar a'Darthar d'Anathar is most welcome to come in and visit."

Karanly jumped up, yanked Ankar to his feet. They were gone.

"My first sister tends toward impulsive," explained Jonathon.

Kraz nodded. "Yes. Sit and talk some. Word says interesting things on House Darthar Na."

So they sat and talked, some.

Outside, Dee nodded goodbye to Kraz and said to Jonathon, "Home first. Then I think House Parthandar.

Jonathon nodded, and said, "Cousin-house Patal is most hidden. I skipped them as I didn't think that one would be able to find and bother them."

Dee and Jonathon walked into a room ready for a meal and found four young women and Karanly already there along with Ankar and three Ice Cats who sat staring with fixed predator eyes at the food.

Tiela was wearing a chain mail shirt similar to that which Armilin wore except it was a soft blue color.

A long, black staff leaned in a corner. Armilin thought that she ought to learn that skill, the art of the staff.

Winala was discussing very intently some minor point of proper behavior for Heads with Eltrill.

Karanly was watching them and smiling, then she smiled at Dee and Jonathon.

Dee sat in an open chair next to her and leaned close and whispered, "Have you all been teasing Ankar. He looks puzzled."

"No. It is just a new experience for him. He is being raised in an all male house."

Dee grinned and began to eat, watching her daughters.

Tiela noticed and nodded her head at her sister and smiled.

Winala had called in a book and was pointing to something on one of the pages for Eltrill to read.

Dee cleared her throat loudly. All eyes jumped in her direction. "All lessons going well? I hope."

Winala grinned. "Most well, Mother." She closed the book and sent it back to the library.

Armilin patted Tiela on the shoulder. "Most well. Very talented."

Tiela smiled. "It is fun."

Eltrill stood and bowed deeply to Dee. "Karanly does say that this one is ready for the duties and obligations of House Head, Princess. May the rest of my family gather here to plan our future."

Dee stood and bowed deeply to her. "It is our

pleasure to do so, Narkalar House Head Eltrill."

She looked at Jonathon who nodded.

"All," said Dee, "are welcome to come in as you may." She beckoned. Ar appeared. "Ar will show you a large gathering room that you may use as long as you require."

Dee sat and nudged Jonathon with a elbow.

He sipped. And nodded.

They casually walked along one of the main halls.

She laughed. "I am really learning a lot about this House Head business. Winala keeps giving me books to read."

He nodded.

"Jonathon?"

He jerked. This was new voice for her to use. "Ummm?"

"Can a second sister become House Head?"

"Yes." He held up his hand, one finger extended. "As long as the first daughter agrees with no tension between the pair." He stopped, turned, and frowned at her.

She smiled. "I just think that Winala would be much better than Tiela as she is, ummmm, not very interested in being that."

"Yesssss. It does appear to be so."

"I will talk with them and see what they think." She started walking again and grumbled, "After we visit House Parthandar first."

He nodded.

The structure was build all along the top of a low ridge in a stark environment of parched and sparse vegetation and loose stone. The building had utilized the same stone as an outer cover to its walls. It was a white-bleached place.

"Ummmm," said Jonathon.

"Really a desolate place."

They worked their way up the slight slope until they arrived at the door.

Dee knocked.

The door swung in.

"Yes?" He was dressed all in black and was somewhat shorter than Dee.

"Daliera and Jonathon come to visit," she said.

He gasped, "You!"

She nodded. "Yep. It's me!"

"Wait." The door slammed shut.

"That's different," mumbled Dee.

"Ummmmm."

So, they waited.

Dee nudged Jonathon. "What is the proper amount of time to wait?"

"Ah ummm. Some small bit more."

"O.K." She leaned against the wall

Finally, the door slowly sung open.

"I an Eandtar, Head, House Parthandar. So, you

choose to visit, finally?"

"Yep." She squinted into the gloom. It was another short male. "May we do that?"

He nodded. "Yes. You may. Do come in."

They walked in. Soft lights turned on as they did. He led them down a hall to the right and then into a room of hard chairs and a heavy wood table. He poured and handed cups to Dee and Jonathon.

"What?"

"Ummmm ah," said Jonathon.

Dee cleared her throat. "Your third son is irritating all of my, ah, cousins, and me, especially me. That son is making wild demands, improper demands, as I have been told, and causing damage to houses."

Jonathon watched Eandtar carefully.

Dee sipped and set her cup down. "This sort of behavior has to stop." She leaned back and took another sip.

Eandatar frowned at her. "You, the female, took his offspring and refused our visit. He has a grenone."

Dee surged to her feet and leaned toward Eandtar. "That creep has a grenone!" She banged her fist on the table. "I didn't agree to have children! I certainly didn't agree to be, ah, fertilized unwillingly!" She glared at him and slowly sat down. "I think that my grievance takes precedence."

Eandtar stared at her. "Behave!"

"What!" She drained her cup, stood, refilled it, and spun around, pointed a finger at him. "Is that rotten

S.O.B. here? In this house? Are you harboring that certifiable lunatic? I want to know?" She waved wildly. Coffee flew in all directions.

One corner of Eandtar's mouth turned down. "You . . . want . . . to . . . know?" He refilled his cup. "How dare you!"

Dee turned to Jonathon, set her cup down, and frowned. "Is there something wrong with this house? Are they all congenitally stupid? Or something?"

Eandtar grabbed her shoulder and spun her around.

She pushed.

He flew across the room and crashed into the wall. Lurching to his feet, he stared at her.

Dee pointed at him. "Stay right where you are, buddy!"

The four hounds appeared and looked around the room and then at Eandtar.

Jonathon stood, took a sip from his cup and handed her a full one. "Strange. Very strange."

She nodded. "Certainly is that all right." She looked at one of the hounds. "Moe, you remember that one that, ummm, snatched me into that tunnel? See if you can find him, please."

The hound trotted from the room and down the hall.

Dee walked over to Eandtar. "How many sons do you have? Any daughters?" She kicked him.

Eandatr, glared at her.

"Manny, do you think that you could take a bite, just a tiny bite? Out of him?"

The hound walked over and began to glow a brighter red, drooling black smoke from its mouth. It sniffed loudly at the man, who was now pressing himself against the wall.

"No," gasped Eantar. "Three sons, two daughters."

Dee leaned close and stared into his eyes. "And I suppose that you think that it is all right if some male should decide to abuse one of your daughters the way that third son did to me? Perfectly fine, just all right? Shall I ask a few males to join us? You can watch."

Eandatr slowly slipped down the wall until he sat. The hound's head traced his progress.

Two young men and two young women ran into the room, Moe trotting at their heels. They clustered around their father and began to ask questions, all at once.

"QUIET!" bellowed Dee. She dropped into a chair and looked at all the eyes looking at her.

"This is really tiring," she sighed. She looked at Jonathon. "Maybe we should leave and start all over again? Some other time?"

"No." He stepped over to the family cluster. "Where is that third son? That one is irritating many. This house is in great danger if it doesn't stop."

She stepped forward. "I am first daughter Arnat. That one is in a hidden room. Come! I will take you."

"Never!" shouted Eandtar, lunging at her.

Dee shoved her palm at him. He struck the wall, bounced onto the table, rolled, and crashed to the floor. And lay still.

"Keep them all where they are," ordered Dee. The hounds all glowed brighter. "Lead on," she said to Arnat. She and Jonathon followed her out the door. Moe followed them.

"I am truly sorry for all this," Dee said to Arnat. "But your brother is crazy."

Arnat nodded. "Spoiled worst. Father taught all of them that males have absolute authority over females. Second sister and I would flee except they would come after us and do horrible."

Dee looked at Jonathon and said, ever so softly, "Soon."

He nodded.

They followed Arnat into a dark hall until they came to the end.

Arnat tapped the wall. "Here."

Dee pulled her back as Jonathon stepped forward. And then Dee and Arnate stepped back some more.

Jonathon kicked the wall into the space beyond.

The short man pushed the rubble aside and staggered upright. "I knew that you would come to me." He smiled at Dee. "You are mine!"

"Sorry. Wrong again."

He snatched a dark weapon and started at her.

"No! I am never that way!"

"Sure you are." She pointed. The ice blast ripped the weapon away. "Again."

Moe blew. The fire ball took the short man back until he crashed into the wall. And burned and burned and burned and burned. And went out.

Arnat walked in and looked down at the blackened spot on the floor. "Nothing left."

"Sorry," said Dee. "I really am."

Arnat turned. "I am not." She bowed. "He was the worst of them all, much the worst." Tears trickled down her cheeks. "I can not remain in this house. We, my sister and I, can not remain in this house."

"Let's go talk with them. First."

Arnat led them back to the room.

Everyone was exactly where they had been when Dee and others had left.

"Let him up," said Dee to the hound standing with one foot on Eandtar's chest.

Eandtar sat up, then stood.

"Sit!" she said to them all.

They did.

She glared from face to face. Jabbing her finger at Eandtar and the two brothers, she growled," You are not going to do anything at all to these daughters, or so help me, I will blow this house into non-existence. Nod, if you understand."

Two brothers did.

Dee stared at Eandtar. He slowly nodded.

Jonathon cleared this throat. "Each of you will now give me your true promise that you will do as Dee just said." He stared at then as they uttered the correct words. "Good. Dee?"

Dee looked at them. "Your daughters cannot stand to live with you any longer." She bowed to Eandtar, then nodded to Jonathon,

"Take us home. All four of us." She nodded. The hounds disappeared.

They were sitting, having a light snack, when Ar walked in.

"Ar, those two sisters are guests for as long as they wish."

One stood and bowed. "Arnat."

Then the other. "Rindle."

"They," said Dee, "are from House Parthandar. No other from that house may enter or are welcome."

Ar nodded. "As you order, Princess, so shall it be. Please come with me, Arnat and Rindle. I know just the rooms. You will like them."

Dee sighed heavily as they left. "Boy, do things ever get complicated in a hurry." She looked at Jonathon. "Does stuff like this go on all the time?"

"No." He sipped from his cup.

Chapter Seventeen

Busman's Holiday.

The Free Floating Mind.

She sat on the small platform on the hard chair, the hard-backed folding chair and watched the people settling down in the rows of similar marginally comfortable folding chairs. She took a sip from the tall paper cup with the paper insulating sleeve slipped around it. And waited.

A tall somewhat slender man, dressed in a pastel pink colored shirt and trousers stepped up to the small podium and cleared his throat.

"Welcome," he began, and waited for them to quiet down. "Welcome to the Free Floating Mind Bookstore and tonight's event. Our guest author is one you all know and have read and enjoyed. Tonight she will answer questions first and then she will read the first two chapters of her newest novel which is quite a departure from her previous numbers of books. This one has new and unusual characters as she begins to explore a new fantasy genre all her own. As it stated on the dust jacket, she wrote this while she was deep in the

Himalaya Mountains on a retreat. When she returned to civilization she was shocked to find that her house had burned down and that she was presumed to have died in the tragic event."

He laughed. "But here she is, alive and well, and writing once again. Please warmly welcome tonight's guest, D. Grant!"

In the midst of the applause, she stepped up to the small podium, shook his hand, and took a sip from her cup, and waited.

Finally she held out her free hand, and smiled at them. "Questions? Before I read?"

Hands shot up.

She pointed at a young woman.

"Miss Grant, why are you the damsel in distress in your new book?"

Dee laughed. "All my other books have had one so I thought it might be fun, and interesting, to be one in my own story." She sipped. "Minor correction to the press handouts and the book jacket. I heard about my house before I returned."

A man waved his hand. "Isn't your male character rather hard on the vampire literature as it is being written today?"

Dee nodded. "I suppose." She grinned. "But then, that is just Jonathon." She winked at the questioner.

And so it went until she halted them so she could start the last part of the evening's presentation. She thought to herself, it really was fun being an author. And hoped that Jonathon wouldn't grumble too much. Even though he had brought her here.

She took a sip, cleared her throat, and began to read.

"Chapter One.

So, This Is How Things Begin.

A Small House Next to the Ocean.

He woke . . . "

General Bits and Pieces

House Darthar

Jonathon - Othara a'Anathor a'Mdator a'Zgura a'Winfa a'Relda d'Darthar - Head of House Darthar, and Lord of the Darthar family, both branches (Darthar and Darthar Na).

Karanly - Karanalador, first sister. She is the Damadon (sort of an Aunt) to Dee's daughters.

Jant - second brother - cross-tie to Nerela, Head, House Tartarnon.

Silneana - second sister.

Hakar - third brother.

Rinil - fourth brother.

Aberly - third sister.

Antel - fourth sister.

House Darthar Na

Dee - Daliera Fontala a'Anathor a'Mdator a'Zgura a'Winfa a'Relda d'Darthar Na. Head of House Darthar Na.

Ar - Ar'ga'da'fazza'din'ban'ahm'na. Dee's Advisor and Teacher.

Tiela - first daughter

Winala - second daughter

The House Beasts of Darthar Na.

Kartar - a great grizzly bear looking animal with thick, light green scales. One of them was named Gooda by Dee when she was a very young child.

The Inferno Hounds - horse sized animals that vaguely look like dogs. The four that are permanent residents of House Darthar Na, Dee named Manny, Moe, Jack, and Peter.

Furleen - lion sized, cougar looking, feline creatures with bronze colored fur and white tiger stripes on their shoulders and neck. Dee named the one of the house, Purr Cat.

Tarken - giant eagle-like birds who stand taller than most men, the pair are called Hack and Jack by Dee.

Sub-Houses of the Darthar

suta Namel

suta Ean

suta Zbtan

suta Dundar

suta Milaton

- who gifted the *Hamel*, the Ice Cats.

suta Ocedaron

suta Farbin

Dee's Cousin-Houses and their Heads.

Dalir - Parlente
Namata - Fam
Induna - Armilin, Anointed One.
Patal - deeply hidden.
Angorson - Pardosh
Anathor - Fraz

About the Author

George R. Mead began to study anthropology in 1962 after being discharged (honorably) from the U. S. Army, Combat Engineers. He eventually received his degrees, a B.A., a M. A., and a Ph. D. in his chosen field. And many years later an M. S. W. in Clinical Social Work. He has worked in aerospace, taught at the college and university levels, worked in a community action agency, ran a restaurant, been unemployed, and worked for the U. S. Forest Service. He is now retired from the work-a-day world but does a certain amount of consulting, writing, and research. He lives seven miles outside of the small town of La Grande, Oregon, with his wife, one cat, and a German Shepard dog named Katy who firmly believes that staring into his face at nine-o-clock in the evening is a statement that popcorn should be made. A new dog joined the house as an eight-week old puppy found by Katy under some brush in the middle of the American Southwest desert. Rez is now weighs 93 pounds (some puppy).

www.ingramcontent.com/pod-product-compliance
Lightning Source LLC
Chambersburg PA
CBHW052019020726
47501CB00004B/1139